LEONIE
GANT

CURSE
THE
PAST

The Harstone Legacy
Book 4

ISBN-13: 978-0-9943999-9-1

To Mike, Samuel and Nicholas.

I didn't think I'd get there, but I had finally reached the point where I was beginning to accept the fact that I may never have the ability to be a witch, despite my supposed heritage. After weeks of training with my aunt I had finally reached the bottom of my initial well of optimism. I could see Flora was frustrated as well. Or I would be able to see her if I wasn't currently encased in crystal. At the moment all I could see was a grayish blob in front of me.

Surprisingly, I didn't feel fear at my current predicament. After all, my aunt was the coven leader and widely believed to be the most powerful witch in the paranormal town of Walker Bay. I was pretty sure that she would be able to get me out of my current predicament, especially as she had been the one who created this trap, all in the name of training me in the art of witchcraft. A goal that was beginning to look more and more futile as we went along. I had seen this crystal trap from the other side when a woman was furious enough at me to break into my home and triggered one of the wards my aunt had placed around my house to protect me. Next thing I knew I had what looked like a witch shaped statue in my home. Until this moment I had believed that I had taken part in a spell to break her out of that particular piece of my magical home security. Since then, my sheer incompetence at all forms of witchcraft had disabused me of that notion.

I frowned at the gray blob in front of me. I was pretty sure she couldn't see me, but I really wanted out of this trap. Sweat was dripping down the sides of my face and I was sure I could hear my heart beating faster in my chest. Despite my earlier belief that I wasn't really bothered by the position I found myself in, I was starting to feel a little tense and my limbs were beginning to cramp up in the confined space.

I wasn't even sure why we were doing this. According to Flora, magic was all around us and witches have an innate ability to sense and even see magic in the air. That's what brought us to this test, an obstacle course that Flora had set up with obvious strands of magic that I should be able to see and follow to avoid the traps. That hadn't work out so well. I didn't see a thing and fell at the first obstacle.

Seriously, what was taking her so long? As the shape that I was reasonably sure was my aunt began to diminish in size, I started to panic. What if leaving me in this crystal tomb was some sort of tough love training? Maybe she thought that making me feel like my life was in danger would shake free some of the magic inside me. My breathing quickened and I strained to fill my lungs with oxygen. The only thing shaking free was a developing case of claustrophobia.

Just when I thought that my heart was going to beat itself out of my chest, I heard a massive cracking sound that echoed through the crystal. I had a panicked thought about shards of glass flying through the air and I slammed my eyes shut.

"Were you planning on opening your eyes anytime soon?" My aunt's voice had a distinct lack of sympathy to it.

I cautiously opened my eyes, only to have everything start spinning in front of me. I tried to quell the nausea that hit me like a tidal wave.

"Over there if you want to throw up." Flora waved her hand in the direction of some trees on the edge of the clearing.

I stumbled over and leaned down, bracing my hands on my knees and willing my stomach to calm down.

"What was that?" I croaked.

"It was a simple obstacle course that we use for teaching our children about magic."

"You do this to kids?" What kind of sick place had I ended up in?

"Well, yes, it's a favorite party game and it teaches them life skills. Of course, for children we set up an obstacle course that has blinking lights instead of a trap when they hit an obstacle."

"Why didn't you do that for me instead of encasing me in a tomb?"

The look Flora gave me spoke volumes. "I didn't want to insult you."

"Next time, please feel free to insult me. I prefer that to being traumatized. What took you so long to get me out?"

Flora frowned. "I was hoping you might be able to break your way out of it. I created it at the lowest possible setting. Even the smallest amount of magic would have destroyed it."

I hated the feeling that I was constantly disappointing her.

"Why is this so hard?" Usually I don't think I'm the kind of person to whine, but today I felt like there should be an exception.

Flora shrugged, a baffled expression on her face. "I have no idea. I don't understand why somebody as powerful as you seem to be can't master the basics." Her shoulders slumped. "I don't think I can teach you."

Ouch, that hurt. When the person who was chosen to be a coven leader at the age of thirteen tells you that you're a lost cause as a witch, it kind of stings. Usually I would say that at the ripe old age of twenty-seven, I was a little old to be starting my apprenticeship as a witch. They always say that you learn better as a child, so you would expect me to be a little slow. I just didn't seem to be learning anything. I walked back to the center of the clearing and flopped down on the ground, letting the warm sun heat the sudden chill I felt run through me.

"Maybe I'm just not meant to be a witch."

My aunt lowered herself onto the ground with a great deal more grace than I had. "If that were true you wouldn't be a cursebreaker."

Aah, yes, my cursebreaker ability. It meant I could surprisingly, break curses. That was it, my one claim to fame. Or it would be if cursebreakers weren't considered so dangerous they'd been outlawed several hundred years ago. At that time there'd been a massacre of cursebreaker families by the ruling Conclave of witches, meaning my anomaly of a power could be a death sentence if anybody found out about it.

In my defense, I hadn't known that I was a witch until recently when I was kidnapped and dragged from my comfortable, normal life as a librarian. Despite the shocking introduction to all things paranormal, I was now a fully-fledged citizen of Walker Bay, a small town on the coast of Maine where on any given day I was likely to see a centaur walking down the main street, and my aunt was desperately trying to teach me how to be a witch. Unfortunately, even rudimentary spells seemed to be beyond me. In the time I had lived in Walker Bay, I had successfully created the grand total of one spell. That spell was a troll doll that when activated could keep conversations private. This was the reason my aunt was deciding that she wasn't up for the job of teaching me basic spellcraft.

"So, what are you suggesting?" I braced myself for her answer.

Flora's eyes softened as if she could sense my unease. "When I was young my mother and sisters weren't overly interested in my upbringing, so I ran a little wild." She smiled at the memory. "When I was ten, I made friends with a hermit that lived deep in the forest."

"You do realize that sounds exactly like the start of a true crime story."

Flora chuckled. "As an adult I am horrified, but as a child it was exciting to have a secret friend that nobody else knew about."

I groaned from the ground. "And it's sounding worse. Please tell me this story has a happy ending that doesn't involve law enforcement."

"I guess that depends on your point of view. I truly believe that the training I got in magic from that hermit is the reason that I was chosen to be coven leader.

"You think she can teach me." Even I could hear the desperate hope in my voice.

"I think he may be the only one who can."

My head popped up. "He? I thought that women were more powerful witches unless you were a part of certain bloodlines." It was probably why my witchcraft abilities were so weak. My father was the one who provided my witch genes. The less said about him the better.

"I didn't say he was a powerful witch, but he is the most knowledgeable person I know when it comes to our craft."

"Wouldn't a powerful witch be better?"

Flora gestured to herself. "I'm the most powerful witch in

this town and I have tried everything I know how to do. You need something that I can't provide."

"Have I seen him at one of the coven meetings?"

"He doesn't belong to any coven. Hermit, remember?"

I looked everywhere but at my aunt. "What if he can't help me?"

Flora patted my knee. "The magic is there. We know this. We just need to find the best way to tap into it."

I wasn't so sure.

2

"*S*o, were you planning on telling me why you were sulking?"

I should have known that my self-imposed exile was not going to last long. I'd spent the last two days confined to home or the library where I worked. After Flora had informed me that she didn't think she could teach me, I had withdrawn into myself for a couple of days and wallowed in my failure. I had avoided my aunt and my friends. I guess a part of me had been terrified that the final proof that I couldn't cut it as a witch was going to drive away the people I cared about the most.

"You don't look great."

Just the kind of thing I always loved hearing, but this morning I couldn't even muster the energy to glare at my friend as she dropped down beside me after navigating her way across my rickety deck.

"I was trying to enjoy my sunrise." I'd always loved watching the sun rise across the bay and I had taken to enjoying it from the deck on the second floor of my house. Despite the fact I was often told the unique area was a death trap, it was the one redeeming feature of the dilapidated structure my aunt had convinced me was habitable.

Tilda leaned back against the wall and eyed me critically. "You don't look like you are going to enjoy anything today. Are you missing your Destined Beloved?"

Yes, I was missing the man who prophecy had said was my soul mate, but that wasn't why I was feeling like the bottom of my world had fallen out from beneath me.

"Flora doesn't think that I'm teachable." I didn't want to see the disappointment in her face, but I couldn't force myself to look away. "I don't know if I belong in this town. Maybe I have too little witch in me."

I saw the way Tilda flinched at my statement. This was the moment of truth. Tilda had become my closest friend in Walker Bay. If she agreed with my statement, then I'd know that I didn't belong here.

"Pull it out."

Not what I was expecting her to say. "What are you talking about?"

"The troll doll, pull it out."

I put my hand in my pocket and withdrew the one and only spell I had managed to accomplish.

"Now activate it."

I was a little taken aback by this new and commanding version of Tilda, but I complied with her request.

"Was there a reason for this?"

Tilda pointed at the doll. "That is proof that you are a witch. Being a witch is not about how strong your power is. It's about heart and determination, which you have in abundance. That doll represents the fact that you don't give up." She looked around as if she was expecting somebody to jump out at us. "I probably shouldn't be telling you this, but I found something out and I think you need to know it."

"That doesn't sound good."

Tilda inclined her head gravely. "It really isn't. I heard that Magister Hartford tried to hack into your privacy spell."

My mouth dried as I tried to remember all the conversations I had used the spell for. None of which I wanted to be overheard by my ex-boyfriend's fiancée.

"She couldn't get in."

I let my breath rush out in relief. "How did you know?"

"Liam told me."

I shouldn't have been surprised. After the Conclave had sent a team of magisters to investigate our fair town, I had noticed Tilda getting friendly with one of them. From the deepening red on her cheeks it seemed I had underestimated how friendly they had become.

"Does he know why she was doing it?"

The look Tilda gave me spoke volumes. "I'd guess it has something to do with you going out with her fiancé."

No way was I going to take the blame for that one. "How was I supposed to know that Julian was engaged since he was a child? Where I come from arranged marriages between bloodlines aren't really a thing. If she wants to blame somebody, she should be taking it out on that lying snake of a fiancé of hers."

Tilda tapped me on the nose and stopped me mid rant. "Much as I would love to continue hearing about how much of a jerk Magister Bernauer is, I think you missed the important part of the information I was giving you."

"What could possibly be more important than a magister who hates me, eavesdropping on my conversations? Surely there are laws against that kind of thing."

"How about the fact she couldn't get through?" Tilda smiled as she saw when the realization hit me.

"But Flora told me that magister's have the ability to break through privacy spells."

Tilda nodded and started stroking the orange hair on the

doll that was the only tangible proof that I had some magical abilities. "They're usually strong enough to do that and a lot more, but this little monstrosity of yours was too tough for her to get through. That should tell you something."

I couldn't help the smile that was stealing across my face. I knew it was silly and petty, but after feeling like a failure I was willing to grab hold of any victory that I could.

Tilda grinned at the obvious change in my mood but then sobered. "You have to know that everybody is talking about the way you and Flora worked on the men of this town when they came down with the plague. We don't know exactly what kind of power Flora used but we all could see that Flora would not have been able to do it without your support. A lot of people are attributing the recovery of their loved ones to the two of you."

That was both a heartwarming statement and utterly terrifying. I wanted to be a witch, but if people were noticing me, it wouldn't take long before I slipped up and somebody discovered my curse breaking abilities. According to everything I had discovered about the paranormal world, that would be bad.

"What are you two doing up here at such a godforsaken time of the morning?"

I was beginning to realize that when my aunt put wards up to protect my house, she only put them up on the inside. It seemed anybody could come up to the deck. A disturbing thought considering it connected to my bedroom. I was going to be talking to her about rectifying that situation.

I watched as two deputies gently made their way across the deck. Pike didn't seem to be having any issues, but then he was one of the dwarf clan. His low center of gravity limited his chances of falling through the rotting timbers. His partner, Deputy Karl Iversen, wasn't faring nearly as well. It seemed ogres had quite the dense body mass, and the deck needed a bit more work before he'd be able to stride across it confidently.

I smiled at the incongruous pair. Anybody looking at them would assume that the ogre was the more bloodthirsty threat. They would be wrong.

"Aren't you two supposed to be protecting the town, not harassing people on their own properties?"

Pike pointed a thumb at Karl. "Deputy Mother Hen here has been worried that he hadn't seen you for a couple of days. The sheriff left him in charge so he's taking on all the responsibilities, including watching over you."

That was just super.

"Speaking of our fearless leader, when's he coming back?"

I lifted my shoulders and tried to pretend that I wasn't hurt by what I was about to say. "I wouldn't know. He hasn't contacted me since the day he left."

I didn't have to be a genius to interpret the expression being shared by my friends.

"Yes, I'm a little upset, but I'll survive the experience."

"Men suck."

I raised an eyebrow at Tilda. Normally I would have expected her to make a comment like that, but today it came from the dwarf deputy with the bushy beard that came down to the middle of his chest.

"Something you want to share with the group?" Tilda asked as Pike dropped down next to us.

"I thought we were having a female bonding session. Isn't that what you're supposed to say in those circumstances?"

I guess that wasn't any more weird than the rest of my life seemed to be.

"I'm sure he has a good reason." Karl flinched at the glares he got from two witches and a dwarf. "Or not. He's a very bad man."

"No, he's not. He's probably just busy." Too busy to send a

text to the woman who was supposed to be his soul mate even though he'd been gone for two weeks. For me, that was a bit of a worrying sign. From the looks on everybody's faces, I wasn't the only one.

"What have you got planned today?"

I could always rely on Tilda to try to turn an uncomfortable situation around.

"I'm supposed to start training with an Arthur McClune this morning. Flora set it up."

Tilda frowned. "I thought Old Man McClune was dead."

"Apparently not," I replied, a little concerned at the certainty in her voice. "Flora left me a message last night that he is expecting me this morning."

"That cranky old geezer is never going to die."

I was surprised at the animosity in Karl's voice. I didn't think there was anything that could get through his professional demeanor.

Pike chuckled. "Didn't he set your car on fire when you trespassed on his property?"

"I barely trespassed," Karl insisted.

"That's not what I heard." Despite Karl's sour look, Pike seemed to be relishing his partner's discomfort. "I heard that back in high school, you and a few of your buddies decided to get a look at Old Man McClune's place. He didn't take too kindly to being disturbed by a group of teenage ogres in the middle of the night."

My embarrassment at being passed to another teacher was quickly morphing into an understandable concern. "He set your car on fire. Doesn't that seem like an overreaction?"

Karl crossed his arms. "Thank you. Everybody else in this town thought we deserved it."

"More likely they just didn't want to go up against the old man," Pike muttered ominously, although he had a gleeful look in his eyes that made me think he was enjoying messing with me. "He's got a reputation."

Tilda patted me on the arm. "You have no reason to worry. If Flora has set up this training for you, he will treat you gently. She would never put you in a position of danger."

"Are you sure about that?" Pike interrupted, looking meaningfully at the decrepit structure that I was renting from Flora. "I mean, look at this place. It doesn't exactly indicate that your aunt is particularly concerned with your welfare."

I hated to admit it, but the man had a point.

3

*L*ike a child on the first day of school, I approached Arthur McClune's house with a mixture of excitement and sheer terror. In the deepest recesses of my mind I hoped that he would hold the answer to the issues I had with magic. However, there was this gaping pit inside of my stomach that made me think that I was putting too much hope in this man. I couldn't get past the concern that my last chance rested with a crazy hermit who lived in the deepest parts of the forest and set fire to the cars of wayward teenage ogres. I took in some deep breaths, trying to calm myself.

"I can do this."

I know, talking to myself isn't exactly the sign of an ordered mind. I raised my hand to knock on the heavy wooden door and then lowered it again, wanting to kick myself for my cowardice. I couldn't believe that I had reached this point. When Flora had asked me to be her apprentice, I figured that I would be flinging spells around in no time at all. Who would have expected that the niece of the most powerful witch in Walker Bay would prove to be a dud when it came to normal witchcraft? All of a sudden, I started to panic. What if this man couldn't help me? Would I be sent packing? I could feel the dread rising in me at the thought of having to leave this town, where, for the first time in my life, I'd felt like I had a shot at a real home.

"Were you planning on knocking or were you just going to stare at my door for the next few hours?"

I turned around too quickly at the sound of the voice behind me and stumbled, falling less than gracefully onto my backside. I should have known this day would not include me keeping my dignity intact.

I looked up into the wrinkled visage of an elderly man with long white hair and a long white beard. From the expression on his face, I could tell that he was not amused.

"Arthur McClune?" He continued watching me silently as I awkwardly scrambled to my feet. "My aunt, Flora Harstone, sent me here. She thought you could help me."

He grunted, turned around, and walked away. I stood on the porch, not entirely sure what I was supposed to do.

He looked back over his shoulder. "Well, are you coming?"

I could already tell this was not going to be fun. I had to walk fast to catch up to him.

"Where are we going?" I queried, wondering why every training session for being a witch seemed to require the equivalent of a gym workout.

"We're heading down to the river."

That was it, nothing else. I followed the elderly man and wondered why it seemed that the senior citizens in Walker Bay were so fit. Between McClune and Flora, I was beginning to wonder if somebody was spiking the water with a fountain of youth potion that kicked in when you turned fifty. I wondered whether there was an age limit before you could start taking it. If not, I was going to start ordering it by the gallon. I hurried to keep up with my companion who didn't seem interested in acknowledging my presence on this little journey. By the time we reached our destination I was starting to get annoyed by the way I was being ignored.

"Why are we here?"

McClune stared at the rushing river as if he barely noticed that I was present. "Why do you think you are here?"

The last thing I signed up for was a therapy session, but my choices were heading down towards zero.

"I believe you're supposed to teach me magic."

McClune snorted as if I'd said something that amused him. "I've got hardly any magic, myself. I'm barely above bound. Trust me, no matter how bad you are, you are not going to learn magic from me."

I was confused. "Then why am I here?"

"Because Flora believes it is your link to the normal world that is stopping you from achieving your full potential. I'm here to teach you about the world you should have lived in."

"I have always been in the world I should have lived in," I didn't like what he was implying. "I belonged with my mother and she could never have been able to stay here. This town would not have allowed it. I would never have stayed in a place that did not accept my mother."

McClune narrowed his eyes. I was pretty sure I had annoyed him, but I'd reached the stage where I no longer cared.

"You are very opinionated."

I stayed silent. He was just stating the obvious.

"Your father was Jasper Harstone."

"That's what I've been told." I wasn't quite sure where he was going with this.

"I remember him. He was an unpleasant child."

"My understanding is that he didn't improve with age."

It was interesting to watch the hermit struggle to suppress a smile at my reply.

"I can see the Harstone in you."

Now, why did he make that sound like an insult?

"Why do you want to learn magic?"

I was a bit surprised at the sudden turn in the conversation. "According to everybody, I'm a witch. Witches are supposed to be able to perform magic."

McClune grunted. "Just because you were born a witch does not mean you can perform magic. In certain cases, it means that it would be better if you didn't perform magic."

I stayed silent. I knew that Flora believed this man could help me, but I was getting the impression that he really didn't want to.

"You belong to the berserker."

That was precisely the wrong thing to say to me. I had to clamp my mouth shut rather than respond the way I wanted to. It seemed the hermit was one of those special people who was gifted in the art of rubbing people the wrong way.

Through gritted teeth I replied as calmly as was possible under these circumstances. "I don't belong to anybody. The Destined Beloved prophecy does not overrule my free will."

He finally turned around and took a real look at me. "I hope that's right, Harstone."

And he just had to take it that one step too far.

"My name is Sadie Goodwin. I do not now, nor do I ever, lay claim to the name, Harstone."

I was surprised at the expression of relief on the man's face.

"There may be hope for you yet, Goodwin."

4

To say that I was relieved for the day to end was a monumental understatement. Once he had decided that I was worthy of his knowledge, Arthur McClune had taken to his role of boring history professor with enthusiasm, or as close to enthusiasm as he seemed to be able to get. I, on the other hand, struggled to stay awake as the warm sun travelled through the sky. Normally I would have enjoyed sitting by a river on a warm day, but the constant drone of a man who seemed to have long ago forgotten that there was joy to be had in life, kind of ruined the moment for me.

Hours later, I was finally released from my torture with barely a wave of the hand. I wasn't entirely sure how much of the mountain of information that had just been dumped on me I was going to retain. I was still a bit hazy on the point of all this, but if Flora thought it would help, then I was willing to try.

After my self-imposed exile for the last couple of days, I was looking forward to getting something to eat at the diner before going home. I called Tilda to see if she could meet me and frowned when there was no answer. In the admittedly short amount of time I'd known Tilda, she was never more than an arm's length from her phone. That included when she was in a magic circle, much to the consternation of the elder members of the coven.

When I walked into the diner, all became clear to me. There, in a booth in the back, sat Tilda, very close to Magister Liam Rigby. When the magisters had come to town to investigate the curse that had almost killed Flora, I had been concerned that they would discover that I was a curse-breaker and haul me back to face the Conclave and the very real threat of death. I had not expected one of them to be an ex-boyfriend, another to be his fiancée, and the third to steal the heart of my best friend. When Julian Bernauer and Penelope Hartford had returned to the Conclave to give their report, I had expected Liam to go with them. He hadn't. Instead he had stayed in Walker Bay, ostensibly to provide a comforting presence to a population that had been traumatized by the upheaval in their ranks, but he seemed to spend more time with Tilda than actually doing anything else. I was happy for her. Really, I was. I was also a little concerned.

Looking around, I could see I wasn't the only one. I slipped into a booth and hurriedly activated my troll doll privacy spell.

"Will you stop glaring at him," I hissed at the agitated werewolf. Normally not something I would recommend doing, but this was a special situation.

"I don't trust him."

I rolled my eyes and wondered how I was going to calm this situation down.

"Of course, you don't trust him. Nobody does, but he's here to stay so we have to deal with the situation."

I felt sorry for Eamon. Being the son of the alpha of the werewolf clan, you would think he could have any woman he wanted. Unfortunately, the woman he wanted was a witch, and there was no way the werewolves would approve.

I slapped my hand down on Eamon's when I heard the growling. "Stop doing that. If you're not willing to step up and claim her, you can't expect her to know what your feelings are. She has a right to search for her own happiness, and if Liam makes her happy, I am not going to let you ruin it."

The anger in Eamon's eyes was swiftly overtaken by pain. "You're right. I'm being selfish."

I sighed at the utter futility of the entire situation. "You're not selfish, you're in love and sometimes that just sucks."

Eamon quirked an eyebrow at me, seemingly pleased to be distracted from his own issues. "Trouble in paradise?"

I snorted. "Like I'm going to tell you."

There was no way I was going to confide in my Destined Beloved's brother that I was feeling neglected.

Eamon frowned. "He didn't say there was a problem when I spoke to him earlier today."

"You spoke to him?" That hurt. I had almost convinced myself that his radio silence was because he was so busy dealing with the Conclave and the Assembly. It seemed I was wrong.

Eamon studied me. "I've said something I shouldn't have, haven't I?"

I plastered a fake smile on my face. "No, everything's fine."

Eamon groaned. "Now I know I've screwed something up. I need you to tell me what it was so I can fix it."

"It's not for you to fix." I swiped my troll doll and stood up. "I'll see you later."

Eamon reached out and stopped me by putting his hand on my arm. "Whatever he did, he doesn't mean to hurt you. Please tell me you know that."

I nodded. "I know."

I did know. The problem was that being subject to a Destined Beloved prophecy wasn't as wonderful as everybody seemed to think. As the Seer had told me, just because the Fates say that you are soul mates, doesn't mean you're still not going to do something profoundly stupid.

I patted Eamon's hand. "Don't worry about it. I'm sure it will be fine."

I walked over to Tilda just as Liam slid out of the booth and I took his place. He grinned at me as he dipped his head and gave Tilda a kiss that increased the temperature in the room a couple of degrees.

"I'll see you soon."

He sauntered off and I focused on the woman who was now going an interesting shade of pink.

"That looks like it's going well."

If it was at all possible, Tilda blushed harder. "It is. Liam is so sweet. I can't believe how wonderful he is."

I smiled. I was truly happy for her. Tilda was one of the kindest and most loyal people I had ever met. To see her so happy was gratifying, despite knowing the pain that Eamon was going through. Speaking of which, I pulled my troll doll out of my bag and activated it. Knowing werewolf hearing like I did, I figured it was cruel to subject Eamon to Tilda gushing about Liam Rigby's many attributes.

Tilda frowned. "Why do we need that?"

"I'm just not interested in our conversation being broadcast to certain werewolves."

Her eyes swept the diner and understanding crossed her face when she saw who I had just left. "You don't want Eamon to know what a jerk his brother is for not calling you."

That wasn't why I did it, but it was as good a reason as any.

"I'm trying very hard not to think about that situation at the moment."

I didn't say that I was successful, but I was putting in the effort.

Tilda's expression morphed from lovesick to concerned friend. "I did tell you he was going to be really bad at the relationship stuff. You can't go from being a man who breezes through women to a Destined Beloved prophecy without hitting a few bumps in the road."

I knew that. I'd had my own problems with the prophecy, but when I'd accepted it, I'd thought that we were both all in. I was discovering that having a berserker werewolf as your Destined Beloved came with its own unique challenges. Number one was a total lack of understanding on his part of how a committed relationship was supposed to work.

"How was your first day with the hermit?"

I could tell Tilda was trying to redirect my thoughts away from the sheriff. I appreciated the attempt.

"I can quite honestly say that I have never met a more boring human being in my life."

Tilda raised an eyebrow. "I thought he was supposed to have all the answers to your problems."

I shook my head. "I think that was the hope, but I'm not exactly seeing how that is going to happen. Today we covered primitive spell castings, the significance of the pyramids and how ancient burial practices included the first ritualized magic."

I grinned at Tilda's perplexed expression and circled my finger in front of her face. "That right there is how I looked, but I had it on my face for six hours."

"I'm really glad it's you and not me."

That did not help me at all. Her phone started ringing and she scrambled in her bag looking for it.

"Now you answer the phone. When I tried to call, all I got was silence."

Tilda frowned as she finally found the phone. "That's weird, I would have known if it had gone off."

I wasn't even going to try to understand the intricacies of a world where technology and magic were combined. From the tone in her voice as she answered the phone, I could tell that something was wrong.

"Don't move, I'll be right there." She dropped the phone into her bag and slid out of the booth. "I've got to get going."

"What's wrong?"

Tilda frowned. "Something weird is happened with my sister. She's at the clinic and wants help."

My heart sank as my mind flashed back to the curse plague that had recently swept through Walker Bay, felling the firstborn sons of the town.

"Are you going to be okay?" I asked.

"Yes," she said, then shook her head. "No. Liam drove me here. Any chance I could catch a lift from you to the clinic?"

I grabbed my troll doll and stood up. "Not a problem." I looked over at Tilda as she chewed on her lip, the suppressed panic obvious on her face. "She'll be okay."

Tilda gave me a weak smile. "Of course, she will. Lisa's tough. She just sounded a bit scared. That's not like her." She paused as if she was looking for some way to explain what she was feeling. "She's my baby sister."

I struggled to find something to say to reassure her. "We'll deal with this."

5

*A*s we pulled up to the clinic, I had to force myself to suppress the shudder of dread that passed through me. When an angry witch had cursed the firstborn sons of Walker Bay, I had spent a lot of time within these walls, trying desperately to halt the progression of the symptoms long enough for us to find the curse tablet and break it. Since then, I had refused to step foot in the building. It looked like that streak was going to be broken far earlier than I wanted it to be.

I followed Tilda through the clinic and winced at the sight that greeted us. Her sister was sitting on a bed with Marigold, the coven healer, beside her. I was grateful to see that she was conscious, but I was shocked by what I saw. Lesions streaked across her face, mostly concentrated around her mouth, like some macabre clown mask. I quickly checked for the tendrils that marked a curse and was grateful when I didn't see any. I knew I had to stop seeing curses everywhere, but my introduction to the paranormal world had been a traumatic one where I had seen the worst of human nature combined with unimaginable power. My thoughts were interrupted by Tilda's horrified gasp at the sight before us.

"What happened?"

Tears poured down her sister's face. "I don't know," Lisa mumbled, her mouth seeming to have difficulty with pronouncing the words. "It just started half an hour ago."

"What is happening?" Tilda demanded of the healer, panic coloring her voice.

Marigold shook her head sorrowfully. "We're not entirely sure yet. Dr Collias will be back soon, and he might be able to tell us something."

As if in answer to our prayers we heard a noisy clattering echoing through the clinic. Who would have thought that the sound of horse hooves against a wood floor would be considered comforting? That's what happens when the town doctor is a centaur.

When Dr Collias entered the room, I marveled at the fact that I was no longer shocked at the sight of a half horse creature with a lab coat and a stethoscope. His keen eyes immediately homed in on his patient, and I was impressed when he didn't wince at the sight of Lisa's face.

"What seems to be the problem, young lady?"

I would have thought the problem was obvious, but then I didn't have a medical degree. The doctor started his examination and, knowing that I had no right to be in the room, I squeezed Tilda's arm and made a hasty retreat.

A HALF HOUR later I was surprised when Dr Collias came out to the waiting room, his whole body radiating tension. "I need you to come to my office."

I jumped to my feet. "Is she okay?"

Collias didn't answer, he simply turned and walked away, evidently expecting me to just follow him.

We entered an expansive room at the front of the clinic and Collias motioned for me to take a seat while he paced across the room.

"Before we start this conversation, I need you to be aware that this room is fully warded and is constantly reinforced. What is said in this room cannot be overheard by anyone."

"Okay." I had no idea where he was going with this.

"Lisa Atwill's affliction is not a natural medical condition. Somebody did this to her and it goes far beyond the harmless pranks that the teenage witches normally play on each other."

My throat clenched at the implications of not only what he was saying, but why he was saying it. "Why are you telling me this? The only reason I'm here is because I gave Tilda a ride."

Dr Collias peered at me over the top of his glasses, a shrewd expression on his face that made me nervous.

"You seem to be forgetting, I was here every moment while you and Flora fought against the plague. I know true power when I see it. I have a feeling that if anybody can help that poor girl in there, it would be you."

I felt my heart speed up as panic took hold. In my head I knew the risks every time I used my curse breaking abilities. I was fortunate in that most people didn't want to entertain the possibility that a cursebreaker could be born spontaneously, especially after the Conclave had so successfully wiped out all the families with the power. I should have known that the centaur who managed to get a medical degree was not most people.

Collias' eyes softened as if he could see the terror his words invoked. "I may not know exactly what you did, but I know that this town owes you a great debt."

I had no idea how to reply. We had gone past the point where he would believe a denial, and my fear of discovery was so great that there was no way that I was going to confirm his accusation, no matter how much I thought I could trust him.

Collias dipped his head as if accepting my unwillingness to confirm or deny his suspicions. "Lisa claims she hasn't been messing with any questionable magic practices which could be the cause of this problem. Both Lisa's mother and grandmother are out of town, so Tilda is the only responsible adult family member available to make medical and legal decisions. I need Lisa's home to be searched and Tilda won't leave her sister. I think you would be the best person to search the house."

"Of course." I stood up abruptly, careful not to look him in the eyes to avoid betraying my fear to him. "I'll contact Flora and see if she can do the search with me."

Before I could get out of the office, Dr Collias grasped my shoulders and turned me around until I was forced to look directly at him. "Please believe that I would never betray you."

I nodded mutely, unsure what to do in this situation. "I'll contact you if we find anything that might be able to help."

With those words I left him standing in his office. I had a feeling things were about to become very complicated.

6

I shouldn't have been surprised when Flora beat me to Lisa Atwill's home. I hadn't been able to hide the panic in my voice when I'd informed her of Dr Collias' request and his suspicions. I activated my troll doll before I even got out of the car. My fears that I had not been careful enough were clamoring loudly in my head. As soon as I stepped towards Flora on the porch, she recognized what I had done and frowned.

"He's a good man. Even if he truly believes his suspicions, he won't tell anybody."

I heard what she was saying, but I couldn't stop the fear that things were getting out of control.

She sighed as she could tell her words weren't making any difference. "I won't let anything happen to you."

I smiled weakly at her attempt to comfort me. We both knew that if the Conclave came after me, there would be nothing she could do to protect me.

Flora straightened her shoulders. "What exactly is happening with Lisa? I didn't quite understand everything you were saying when you called me. We must have had a bad line."

It was kind of Flora to try to make me feel better. The truth was that I had been panicked and incoherent, trying to explain the situation with Lisa while blending it with my fear that everyone was going to work out that I was a curse-breaker. As a result, our conversation had been a garbled mess.

I drew in a deep breath and focused on the important matter at hand. "Lisa Atwill was admitted to the clinic about an hour ago. She has lesions all over her face, mostly around the mouth area. I didn't see any evidence of a curse on her, but Dr Collias has his concerns."

"Ambrose is smart," Flora said as she pressed her hand flat against the front door. "If he thinks there is something magical involved in this case, we would be wise to listen to him."

The door sprung open and I followed my aunt inside. She looked at me expectantly. "What do you see?"

My eyes swept the room we were in. It was a lived-in home. Clothes were scattered around the place and dishes were in the sink. In short, this was a house where a teenager had been left alone while her parent was away. I had no doubt that the plan was for there to be a frantic cleanup in the final hours before her mother was due home. I was sure that wasn't what Flora was asking.

"There's nothing here that I can see. Everything looks completely normal." My eyes were drawn to the stairs. "The marks on her face were too personal. If we're going to find anything it will be in her bedroom or some place that is exclusive to her."

I was already making my way up the stairs as I finished talking. When we got to the first floor, I could feel a slight nausea creeping up the back of my throat. I fought the urge to spit.

"There's something up here."

I found myself following a feeling and opened the door to Lisa's bedroom. At first glance it looked like any other teenage girl's room. It even had some posters of boy bands that I could recognize. Apart from having questionable taste in her music preferences, my first sweep of the room found nothing. I grimaced as I realized that the next step in the search was going to be a great deal more invasive than I had been hoping for.

"I need to go through her things," I announced. "I'm feeling that there's something here. I'm just not sure what it is."

Flora nodded without saying a word. I had a feeling she didn't want to distract me from my quest, distasteful as it was. My first act was to drop to the floor and look under her bed. Grateful not to find anything, I stood up and started a methodical search of the room with my aunt watching from the doorway, a concerned expression on her face.

"I'm not going to fall apart on you." I hated the fact that I caused her so much worry. "Although, if I had a vote, I would have much preferred to have Maude's ability."

Tilda's grandmother had the power to manipulate the weather. My introduction to the world of witchcraft had been watching her create a ball of lightning in her hand. One of the most impressive things I'd seen, and in the last few months I'd seen a lot.

Flora nodded. "I can understand that," she said, "but as one of the over hundred people whose lives have been saved by your ability, I'm pretty grateful for what you can do."

I nodded sharply at her words and continued searching. I could feel the nausea growing, so I knew I was close to finding something. I started going through her makeup bag and flinched when I found what I was looking for. I pulled it out and held it up.

"What is that?"

I peered at the small jar. "I think it's lip balm, although it doesn't look like one that you'd normally buy at the shop."

Flora reached for the jar and I pulled it back.

"You don't want to do that."

Understanding dawned on Flora. It was sometimes difficult to remember that she couldn't see what I saw. For example, at the moment she saw an innocuous small jar, half full of some yellowish substance that I normally wouldn't look twice at. I, on the other hand, saw two black tendrils wrapped tightly around the container, showing that somebody had decided to put a curse on a jar of lip balm to be used by a teenager. I shook my head in disgust. What was the world coming to?

I touched the tendrils and watched them disintegrate before sitting down on the floor.

"What are you doing?"

I looked up to see Flora's confusion at my actions.

"I'm going to destroy this thing."

Understanding dawned on her face. Other times when she had witnessed my breaking of curses, I had ended up passing out and dropping to the ground. I had learned to minimize the distance that my head had to hit the floor. Despite my natural inclination to destroy this thing as quickly as possible, I drew in a deep breath and concentrated on it in an attempt to discover who had cast the curse. Usually at this point, I was assailed with images or whispers of power. Flora and I were working on the assumption that because it cost a piece of a witch's soul to cast a curse, the curse became almost sentient and would promise me anything to survive. With the past few curses I had broken, the promises would start out with a seduction of power and would end with vows of retribution.

This time there was silence. I frowned as I felt nothing coming from the lip balm. Hoping for a reaction I lifted it high above my head. When nothing happened, I threw it as hard as I could against the wooden floor. Finally, there was something. It was just a flash of an image, but it was enough to tell me that this curse had not been set randomly. For some reason a sixteen-year-old girl had been targeted. Glancing over to where the jar had hit the floor, I could see that it had smashed into dust exactly like every curse tablet I had destroyed. Just when I thought I was beginning to understand curses and this ability of mine, someone sent me a curveball.

I looked up into Flora's understandably confused face.

"That was a little underwhelming," she said.

I pulled myself up and dusted off my jeans. "We need to talk to Lisa."

DR COLLIAS WAS WAITING at the front of the clinic to greet us.

"Whatever you did, it worked." The doctor's voice was pitched low as if understanding my desperate need for discretion. "The lesions have completely disappeared. She is able to talk properly and there seems to be no lasting effects. I'm keeping her in overnight, but that's purely as a precaution. Unless you have some information I should be aware of, I will be releasing her tomorrow morning."

Flora glanced at me quickly and I gave her a slight nod.

"I think that will be fine," she said. "We do need to speak to Lisa."

Despite her attempt to protect me from getting too much attention, I could see that the doctor wasn't fooled, and he looked straight at me. "Is there something I should be aware of?"

I straightened my shoulders and returned his gaze. "We don't know yet. If there is, we will let you know the second we do."

Dr Collias searched my face and must have seen something there.

"Very well." He turned and walked back into the clinic.

We followed him into Lisa's room to find a petulant teenager now complaining loudly about the fact that she couldn't go home.

"Lisa."

At Flora's commanding tone Lisa stopped talking.

"We found some issues with a lip balm in your bedroom. Is there anything you can tell us about that?"

Lisa frowned as she concentrated as if trying to remember, until a flush of red raced across her cheeks. "Was it the one in the jar?"

"Yes." I leaned forward, hoping that she would be able to shed light on how she came to be in possession of cursed lip balm. Even as I thought it, I knew it sounded ridiculous.

"I bought that three years ago from a Traveler." She looked up at us. "She promised me it would give me bigger lips. I don't use it that often, but I did today because I was meeting some friends and…"

Her voice trailed off, but we could fill in the blanks. Now that our attention was no longer focused on lesions on her face, we could see the perfectly done hair and makeup. Lisa had clearly got ready with a specific person in mind. Unfortunately, it looked like her plan had backfired in a spectacular fashion.

"Are you saying that you've used this lip balm before?" I asked.

Lisa nodded. "I guess I've used it about ten times over the

last three years. It's usually pretty effective and it just gives me bigger lips without needing to get fillers."

"And you've never had a problem before?"

Lisa shook her head. "Sometimes when I get things from Travelers, they don't work so well, but this one worked great."

"Are you saying her lip balm did this to her?" I could understand the incredulous tone in Tilda's voice. If I hadn't seen the familiar tendrils on the jar, I wouldn't have believed it myself.

"I believe so," Flora inserted smoothly. She turned her attention back to Lisa. "Is there anybody that you can think of who might do this to you? It might not have been malicious. It could have been a prank that went just that little bit too far."

Lisa shook her head. "Nobody I know would do this to me. Anyway, that lip balm has been at the back of a drawer, buried under piles of makeup for ages. It was totally random that I would use it."

"If I get my hands on whoever did this…"

It wasn't often that I saw Tilda angry, so this was quite the experience. At least this time it wasn't aimed at me.

"Let's just remain calm," Flora soothed. "We need to work out why this happened and how. Going off without knowing all the facts is not going to help anyone. We need to approach this in a methodical manner." She gave Lisa a stern look. "I want a list from you of anyone who may be upset with you at the moment, and that includes Cleo."

Lisa started to protest but Flora put up a hand. "I know she's one of your best friends, but I also know that you've both been competing for Aaron's attention. At this stage we can't rule out any motivation. I also want this list to include anybody who has been at your house recently."

Lisa looked rebellious but nodded her head in submission to her coven leader. Flora indicated for me to join her.

"Tilda, I will be expecting that list in the morning. Make sure it is done. You can pass it to Sadie when you meet for breakfast."

I had to suppress a smile at the way Flora seemed completely at ease with organizing everybody's life. I could see that Tilda was struggling to hide her amusement as well. At least it blunted the anger she was feeling.

Flora looked sternly at Lisa. "I want you to rest a couple of days. If at any point you feel that something isn't right, you are to call me immediately. Do you understand, young lady?"

Lisa nodded, all signs of rebellious teenager cowed under the power of the coven leader.

We left Lisa with her sister and went back to our cars. I activated my troll doll because I had questions that I didn't want anybody to overhear.

"What is a Traveler?"

Flora smiled. "I was wondering how long it was going to take you before you started asking questions. A Traveler is a wandering witch who goes from town to town and sells potions or artifacts."

I frowned. "According to Lisa, she bought the lip balm when she was thirteen and she's used it several times over the last three years, all without any issues at all." I looked over at Flora and stated what had been bothering me about this entire situation. "I know teenagers can be a bit annoying, but sacrificing a part of your soul simply to mess up her face seems to be a bit of an overreaction."

Flora sighed and leaned back against her car. "You're right. Normally I would say that it wasn't possible and that it may have just been a spell that would have worn off in a short period of time. If it wasn't for you, we wouldn't even know that it was a curse." She scrubbed a hand over her face. "I think I need to talk to the Seer. The curses that have been hitting Walker Bay recently have been understandable. Horrifying, but at least I can comprehend why it happened. Cursing a child's makeup, I can't even begin to fathom the mind behind that."

I grasped her hand, concerned she was working herself into a state. "We'll figure it out," I said, trying to inject my voice with a confidence I didn't necessarily feel.

Flora smiled sadly. "Maybe, but I shudder to think what we will find."

7

*T*he next morning found me sitting on my deck watching the sun rising over the town. I used to enjoy the view from a park bench that looked out over the bay until a murderer had threatened to kill me and leave pieces of my body scattered around the park. Since then, I hadn't been able to return to that place without feeling a ball of fear settling in my stomach. I was finding my deck provided the peaceful setting I craved to start the day.

I sighed and closed my eyes when I heard footsteps coming up the derelict stairs on the side of the building.

"I'm fine, Deputy," I called out, sure that my early morning visitor had to be one of Walker Bay's finest, checking up on me for my absent Destined Beloved. "You can make your report and you might want to tell him that calling me directly would have been the better way to go." I paused and thought about what I'd just said. "No, wait, don't do that." The last thing I wanted was for Conall to know how upset I was at the fact he hadn't contacted me.

"Is your Destined Beloved neglecting you?"

I jumped at the rumbling tones of a voice I didn't think I

was ever going to hear again, quickly glancing down to ensure I was completely covered. I hadn't expected any visitors when I came out on the deck for my morning ritual and wasn't exactly dressed for entertaining. Especially an ex-boyfriend who didn't believe a Destined Beloved prophecy was as final as everybody else did.

"What are you doing here, Julian?"

Magister Julian Bernauer frowned as he peered around at the deck. "This thing is a death trap."

"That seems to be the consensus," I sighed as I watched him carefully make his way over to me.

"I can't believe your Destined Beloved is willing to risk your life by letting you stay here."

Usually people blamed my aunt for the state of the house. A fair accusation seeing as she was the owner and my current landlady. Of course, Julian would see it as an opportunity to take a dig at the man who had replaced him.

"How's your fiancée?" I asked.

See, I could play this game too. I had recently discovered that while we were seeing each other, Julian had not only been hiding the fact that he was a witch, he had also been hiding an arranged betrothal from when he was a child.

Julian grimaced. "You know it means nothing. I'm currently in the process of getting the engagement nullified."

"Why would you do that?" I was truly perplexed at his statement. From what I understood, Julian and his fiancée were both from high ranking witch families. In a world where bloodlines were all important, they were considered a match made in political heaven.

"I won't marry her if there is a chance I can be with you."

He reached a hand out to stroke my cheek and I lurched backwards, smacking my head against the wall I was leaning on. I waved him away as he tried to help and gestured between us with the hand that wasn't clutching my aching head.

"We are never going to happen. I've told you that repeatedly. Why do you keep persisting in saying that we will?"

Julian smiled sadly as he sat down next to me. "Because I truly don't believe that you belong with the berserker. I miss what we had together."

"You were the one who walked away," I reminded him.

"And I regret that decision every day."

He looked like he wanted to say more, but he was interrupted by another visitor who thought nothing of injecting themselves into my quiet time.

"Son, I would suggest you start walking, because you are doing some serious damage to your life expectancy."

I couldn't help the smile that erupted on my face at the arrival of the defender of my virtue. I could always depend on Pike not to mince his words and to advocate violence.

Apparently, Julian was not impressed by the interruption. "I don't see how it is any of your business, Deputy," he sneered.

Pike smiled in a way that told me he was expecting a confrontation and was looking forward to it. "Anything to do with Sadie is my business, even if she wasn't soul bonded to my boss, which she is, in case you missed the memo."

I did not like the expression on Julian's face.

"I got the memo. I just don't believe the Seer's dictates should be followed as slavishly as the rest of you do."

I winced at his statement. Since I'd been dragged into Walker Bay, it had been drummed into me that the Seer's word was law. I may not have liked it, but I had learned to accept it.

Pike leaned back against a post and I hoped it held. "This is going to be entertaining."

I wish he hadn't made that statement with quite so much relish.

Julian looked over at me. "Enjoy your day. I'll see you soon." He stood up and started to make his way to the stairs, taking very careful steps.

I frowned as a thought hit me. "What are you doing here, anyway? I thought the investigation was complete. Liam's been mopping up the final details."

Julian gave me a smile that I didn't trust at all. "The Conclave feels that Walker Bay needs some attention. My team has been stationed here indefinitely until we work out what is going on in this town." He looked over at the house next door. "I'm your new neighbor for the foreseeable future."

Until this moment I had thought there was plenty of room between my place and my nearest neighbor. Now that I knew my neighbor was a magister for the Conclave, the same organization that had hunted cursebreakers to extinction, it felt like he was living right on top of me.

Pike waited until Julian had started to make his way across my yard into what was now his home. "You really do make life interesting for the rest of us, don't you?"

I truly wished I didn't.

8

I'd finally managed to convince Pike that I didn't need twenty-four hour protection to deal with the magister that was living within perfect stalking distance of my house. I was going to ignore the entire situation for now. Not exactly the healthiest way that I could deal with it, but it worked for me.

I could tell from the look on Tilda's face when I arrived at the diner that she had already heard about my predicament. Without saying a word, I gave my breakfast order to the waitress and then pulled out my troll doll and activated it.

"Pike or Liam?"

She grinned at my question. "I was on the phone with Liam telling me when a message came through from Pike." Tilda studied me. "Puts a bit of a wrinkle into the situation, doesn't it?"

I shrugged. "Doesn't make any difference to me. It was a little bit of a shock though."

"According to Liam, Julian pushed to be stationed here. He could afford any house in this town, but he specifically looked for the closest one to you. He's currently breaking his engagement to Penelope Hartford and that is really rare for those families." She drew in a breath. "His father's family is furious, and Violet and Myra are apoplectic. They blame you."

That was just great. I was now on the radar of high-ranking members of the Conclave, not to mention this gave one of the leaders of the Path coven and her daughter yet another reason to dislike me. Although, to be honest, I was never going to be one of Violet and Myra's favorite people.

We stopped talking when our breakfast was delivered, but as soon as the waitress stepped away, Tilda returned to the matter at hand.

"The sheriff is going to lose his mind when he finds out. How are you going to deal with that?"

I shrugged. "It's not like he has any say in the matter and I have no idea when he's returning. For all we know he might be gone for another month or more. Whatever is happening here could be over before he returns."

Tilda twirled her fork in the air. "I like your optimism, but if you believe that he is going to stay away when he hears his rival is living next door, you are seriously deluded."

Whatever I was going to say next was interrupted by an argument that was starting in a booth across from us. I hadn't really noticed the two teenage boys when I had come into the diner, but as their voices grew louder, they became the focus of everyone in the building. I could see the perplexed expression on Tilda's face.

"What's going on?" I whispered, despite the fact I could have shouted at the top of my lungs and nobody would have heard what I was saying through the privacy bubble.

"That's Aaron Pixton and Benton Westcotte. They've been friends from the moment they were born." She frowned as we watched one of the boys lurch across the table and grab the other boy's collar. "I've never seen them have a cross word with each other."

At the point where it looked like actual violence was going to happen, a couple of men stepped up and grabbed hold of the struggling boys. I was surprised to see Eamon stride into the diner, anger on his face.

"What is going on?" he roared, frustration evident in his expression.

I had wondered how much power Eamon had as the eldest son of the alpha. From the way every werewolf in the diner bowed their heads, it looked like a lot.

He pointed at the two boys. "You two. Outside. Now."

I was surprised by the defiant looks the boys were giving Eamon. My understanding was that the dominance hierarchy of the werewolf clan was absolute. I didn't think even teenage rebelliousness could break through that. I felt a slight pressure around me and watched as the insolent expressions gave way to compliance. Unlike his father who used the dominance power indiscriminately, Eamon targeted it at the two boys. I could see the admiration from the other werewolves that they weren't driven to the ground by an arrogant leader. Conall kept telling me that Eamon would one day make the best alpha the werewolf clan had ever seen. After this display of judicious power, I was inclined to believe him.

As the two boys were dragged out, Eamon approached our table. "Are you okay?" he asked.

Despite the query being made of both of us, his eyes were trained on Tilda.

She nodded. "It didn't get a chance to go far before people stepped in." She frowned as a thought occurred to her. "How did you get here so fast?"

Eamon scrubbed a hand down his face. "We've been having issues with some of the younger members of the clan and I've been putting out fires all morning. Seems the football team is not leaving all of its aggression on the field."

Walker Bay had a football team? How had I missed that?

He glanced through the window to see the boys still arguing and I could see he was itching to knock their heads together. "I'd better deal with this."

With a last glance at Tilda he walked away. I marveled at the fact she was so oblivious to his feelings for her.

As I finished eating my breakfast, I noticed something which seemed to have been knocked to the floor during the altercation between the two boys. My heart plummeted when I realized what I was looking at. Glancing around the diner I noticed that everybody's attention was taken by the sight of Eamon tearing a strip off the boys. I pushed my phone off the table and hoped that the military grade case I'd paid extra for lived up to its hype. I leaned down and swiped the object up with my phone. I came up to find Tilda watching me.

"What are you doing?"

I held up my phone, grateful that the screen was still intact. "I knocked this." I quickly pushed the phone and the object behind it in my bag and stood up. "I need to get going to work."

Tilda frowned when she looked at my plate. "But you're not finished."

There was no way I was going to be able to eat another bite. "I'll be fine. I'm not really hungry, anyway." I paused as a thought struck me. "Do you have that list that Flora asked Lisa to put together?"

Tilda nodded, confusion at my sudden change in behavior evident in her expression. "My sister was not happy about it, but we got there eventually."

She pulled a sheet of paper out of her bag and passed it to me. I didn't even look at it before shoving it into my bag.

"I'll see you later."

I blindly left the diner, not even glancing at the two boys still being reprimanded by Eamon. I just kept my head down until I got to my car. Once inside, I called Flora.

"You need to meet me at the library. I think we have a problem."

9

*F*lora found me in the coven library, sitting at a desk, examining a ring.

"What are you doing?"

"I'm wondering why the teenagers of this town have decided to start using cursed objects in their everyday life."

Flora sat down on the chair opposite me. "What are you talking about?"

I held out the ring that I had been studying. "This just fell off the hand of a teenage boy who was arguing with his friend in the diner. Until I grabbed it, there were tendrils coiled tightly around it. They disintegrated in my hands, but I'm just curious why this is the second innocuous object with a curse on it that we've found in the possession of a child in the past two days."

"Can I look at it?"

I held it close to her. "I'd suggest not touching it. I have no idea what this thing does, and I probably won't until I destroy it."

Flora squinted at the ring. "This looks like one of the rings that the football team got when they won the championship last season." She gave it a closer look. "Do you know whose it is?"

I twirled the ring around. "I think it belongs to either Aaron Pixton or Benton Westcotte. They started fighting in the diner this morning before being hauled out. I found this on the floor after they were gone. I'm thinking it fell off one of them during the altercation."

Flora frowned. "That doesn't sound right. Aaron and Benton are lovely boys. They've never caused their parents any trouble before."

"Well they were making up for lost time today." A thought struck me. "Eamon said he'd been dealing with issues from other football team members all morning. Something about them being aggressive."

Flora groaned. "Please tell me you're not thinking that the whole football team could be affected by this."

I wish I could. "I'm just saying it's a possibility we might want to look at."

Flora rubbed her hand over her face. "At least half of that team were werewolves. If Aidan finds out that those boys are the victims of a witch's curse he will go on a rampage."

I closed my hand around the ring. "Then we will have to fix this problem in a way that he never finds out."

I squeezed my hand as I concentrated on the ring. Once again, I got a brief image, and then I was surprised when the ring disintegrated.

"What just happened?" Flora looked as perplexed as I felt.

"I'm not entirely sure." I opened my hand to find a fine layer of dust stuck to my palm. "I'll be right back."

I made a quick trip to the bathroom and scrubbed my hands clean. On the way back to Flora I snagged a bottle of sanitizer that I had taken to carrying around with me and liberally coated my hands. I had no proof at all that any of this helped to clean away any part of the curse, but it made me feel slightly better.

"You know that isn't going to make any difference," Flora said wryly.

"We don't know that," I said as I rubbed my hands together. "For all we know, my need to disinfect may be making me stronger. It could be the reason I'm having less problems destroying these curses than I've had with previous ones."

"Do you really think that's the reason?" Flora looked dubious.

I shook my head. "No, these latest curses are nothing compared to the previous ones I've dealt with. If I didn't see the tendrils which mark them as a curse, I would think that they were prank spells the teenagers were playing on each other. There seems to be no malice or real purpose to them. Although the effects seem pretty severe for a prank."

"What did you see when you broke it?"

I sighed, frustrated at the whole situation. "I didn't see much of anything, just the boys celebrating what must have been the championship win. I didn't feel anything. It's like whoever cast this curse is not really invested in it. When I've broken other ones, I can feel the hate, the rage and the evil involved. They seethe with it. This one, and the one from yesterday, are giving me nothing." I pulled out the piece of paper that Tilda had given me. "Here are the names that you asked Lisa for."

Flora read through the names and frowned.

"What's wrong?" I queried, not liking the look on her face.

"Did you look at this list?"

I shook my head. "I was too focused on the ring. I just shoved the list in my bag."

"The names I have here include Aaron Pixton, Benton Westcotte, Cleo Moore, Doran Pearson and Bryn Pritchard."

I grimaced. "That can't be good, can it?"

Flora shook her head. "If three members of that group are victims of a curse, the chances of the others also being victims is quite high. Doran's a member of the football team as well."

"How many of that list are witches?"

Flora paused at my sudden query. "Doran and Bryn. Why do you want to know that?"

I stood up. "Because our chances of getting answers are better with witches. If we try to interview werewolves we're going to have to deal with Aidan, and I really don't have the will to take on the werewolf alpha today."

As I EXPECTED, it was easy for Flora to organize meetings with the two witches and we were soon sitting opposite a sullen teenager.

"I haven't done anything wrong."

Even if I hadn't seen the ring on his finger with tendrils twined around it, I would have been able to tell that the hostility that Doran was showing was out of character just by the bewildered expression on his parents' faces.

I smiled at the recalcitrant teenager. "That's an interesting ring you have there. Could you tell me where you got it?"

He hesitated and I could almost see that he was debating whether he should answer at all. I hoped that he was strong enough to fight the effects of this curse.

"Why should I talk to you? You're a null. Everybody says so. You shouldn't even be in the coven." He jerked a thumb at Flora. "If she wasn't your aunt, you wouldn't even be allowed in this town."

The swift intake of breath from Doran's parents should have indicated to him that he'd taken things too far. I really hoped it was the curse making him act like this, but considering he was a teenager, I couldn't be sure. I could feel Flora was attempting to calm the situation by applying a small amount of dominance power. It wasn't working, and from the annoyed look on her face I could tell that Doran was about to get a reminder about the perils of going up against a coven leader.

Before she had a chance to calm the situation in a moderate way, Doran made a potentially fatal mistake. He surged upward and towered over me in a threatening stance.

"Get out of my house. I'm not going to talk to you and if you keep asking questions, you'll be sorry."

Before anybody could react, Flora took control. Doran dropped to the ground, his hands covering his head.

"I would suggest you keep your distance from my niece and never question her right to be at my side."

The restrained anger in Flora's voice chilled everybody in the room. I could see the terror in the eyes of Doran's parents. They knew in that instant that their son's future was precarious. I stood up quickly and slipped the ring from his finger, destroying the tendrils as I clasped it in my hands.

Slowly, by degrees, I could see Flora's power receding. Doran's hands let go of his head and he looked up, confusion in his eyes.

"What's happening?"

That answered one question. It looked like the curse was on the object, not the child themselves. Although, considering it was placed on a football championship ring, it looked like the curse wasn't completely random either. Somebody had to know which kids were getting these rings.

Flora nodded to the parents and they raced forward to help their son sit back on the couch.

"We have reason to believe that there is a spell on the ring you were wearing that increases your level of aggression," she explained. "It seems to have had some unexpected consequences."

Thanks to the relatively minor nature of the magic involved, Flora had informed me that we would be able to play off the effects as a spell rather than a curse. The hope was that nobody would look too deeply into our explanation.

"Why would anybody do that?" Doran's mother looked confused as she stroked her son's hair.

"Believe me, we are working out why this has happened." The steel in Flora's voice sent a shiver down my spine. "What we need to know is where the boys got these rings."

Doran's father raised his head. "The coach gave them out after the championship game last year. It was the first time Walker Bay had won in decades."

"I remember," murmured Flora. She looked down at the shivering boy. "When did you start noticing him acting like this?"

Doran's father shrugged. "It's just been in the last day. We thought it was just him being a teenager." His eyes pleaded with Flora. "If we'd thought for one moment that he had reached the point where he would challenge the right of the coven leader, we would have come to you immediately." He lowered his voice as he looked at Doran with love. "What he just did, that is not our son. He has his moments, but he understands the structure of the coven."

Flora's eyes softened and she stood up and put a gentle hand on Doran's head. "His actions today will not be held against him. I would suggest a cleansing spell to assist in wiping away any lasting effects. In the meantime, we will be taking the ring and will investigate why this has occurred." Her voice strengthened. "I would also suggest you not tell anybody what has happened here until we have more information."

After we left and got in the car Flora turned to me. "I'm assuming you still have it."

I opened my hand to show the ring. The tendrils were gone but I knew the only way to completely free Doran was to destroy it. Without another word I squeezed my hand shut and felt it disintegrate. It was a strange sensation knowing that with cursed objects I had the physical strength to turn a metal object into dust. I was a long way from understanding how all of this worked. I opened the door and partially got out, wiping as much of the dust off on the grass as I could. My aunt went into the glove compartment and handed me a napkin to assist in the process.

"Are we still going to talk to Bryn?" I asked as I worked at cleaning my hands.

Flora smiled. "If we want a better idea as to what is happening with this group of teenagers, I think that would be a good idea."

*W*hen we started talking to Bryn, I began to understand why Flora had smiled. Unlike Doran, Bryn was a veritable font of information and she liked to talk.

"Lisa is totally in love with Aaron, but we all know there is no way he'll risk getting involved with a witch. Cleo thinks she has a clear shot at him, but Aaron isn't interested. Benton wants Cleo but she thinks he's going to be too low on the dominance hierarchy for her future. In reality, the guys are more interested in football at the moment to make any kind of decisions. The coach thinks the team has a real chance of winning back-to-back titles which would be great, seeing as our generation is the first one to win a title in like a hundred years." She frowned and I really hoped she took a breath before she passed out. "Or it could be decades. I don't know. I just know it was a really long time ago. At the beginning of last year we didn't think we had a chance, we kept losing, but then the guys really stepped up and we won every game in the run up to the championship. It was so awesome when we won."

Flora put out a hand to stop the running commentary. "I was there, I remember the game, and yes it was wonderful. What we want to know now, is there a possibility that anyone in your group would target Lisa with a prank?"

Bryn looked as if she was concentrating really hard. "Cleo has a really weird relationship with Lisa. I mean, they're friends but sometimes she gets really competitive. And she does not like that Lisa and Aaron get along so well. She's really against any possibility of a werewolf and a witch together." All of a sudden Bryn focused on me. "She lost her mind when the sheriff ended up with you, but she's kind of accepted it since he got kicked out of the clan and he's not a real werewolf, and you're a null so it's not like you're a real witch."

I sat there, stunned at the way the conversation had gone.

Flora interrupted the stream of consciousness with one word. "Bryn."

For the first time since she had opened the door to us, Bryn fell silent.

I decided to jump in at the opportunity. "About three years ago Lisa bought a lip balm from a Traveler."

"The one that gives her pouty lips," Bryn interrupted. "That stuff is amazing. She let me use some once and my lips never looked so good. I wish I'd got some, but I got the stuff that makes my nose look smaller instead. It works good but these days I'm more likely to use makeup for contouring."

Flora held up a hand. "Are you telling me you've got something from that same Traveler?"

Bryn nodded enthusiastically.

Flora put a hand to her head as if she was beginning to get a headache. "Could you please bring it down to us, we'd like to have a look at it."

Bryn bounced up from the couch and raced up the stairs.

It wasn't long before she was downstairs again. She walked towards Flora with her hand outstretched.

"Here it is, I've used about half of it and it works really well…"

She stopped talking when I stepped between her and Flora and snatched the jar out of her hand. The sight of her about to pass the jar covered with tendrils to my aunt overcame my usual sense of discretion in these areas.

"Thank you, Bryn," Flora said smoothly. "We're a bit concerned as Lisa's lip balm caused some terrible lesions. We're looking to see if a prank has been played or whether there is a flaw in the spells used to make these items."

Bryn nodded her understanding, still watching me carefully. "I didn't mean to upset you by calling you a null. I'm really sorry if I hurt your feelings."

I gave her a small smile. "It's okay. I'm not upset."

Bryn seemed relieved. "I hate upsetting anyone." She frowned as a thought seemed to come to her. "You might want to talk to Cleo. She was with us the day we bought those things. I didn't see her buy anything, but I remember she was looking really hard at some hair removal cream." She lowered her voice. "Cleo has had issues with excess hair for years. I'm not sure if it's a werewolf thing but her body hair seems to grow back quickly no matter what she uses. She's always looking for something new that will help."

"Is there anything you can tell us about the Traveler?" I asked trying to steer the conversation to information that might be more pertinent.

I could see Bryn concentrating as she tried to pull back on a memory. "She was kind of young, really pretty. Usually you think of Travelers as being old and grumpy, but she was really friendly. She was happy to talk to anybody about anything. I remember Coach Weber was there too and he was talking to her for a long time. I think he was looking for a present for his wife."

I glanced over at Flora and saw she'd picked up on the reference to the coach again.

"Did you get her name or where she came from?"

I shrugged when Flora glanced over at me. Bryn seemed to be the outgoing teenager who talked to everybody she met. If anyone was going to get information from random strangers it would be her.

Bryn screwed up her face in concentration. "You know, I don't think she had a name, or not one I remember."

"That's fine," Flora said smoothly as she stood up. "You've been a great help."

Bryn beamed at her coven leader's praise. "Can you get the cream back to me when you've finished looking at it? I do like the way it makes my nose look smaller."

I glanced down at the half empty jar which was covered with black tendrils. "I would suggest you stick with contouring."

BACK IN THE car I destroyed the cream.

"You know what disturbs me the most?" I said mildly as I went through the ritual of cleaning my hands. "Why are thirteen-year-old girls buying untested creams from a random traveling salesperson to give themselves a duck pout and a nose job?"

Flora sighed. "Is it really so different in your world?"

I guess not.

"Where do we go now?" I asked. "From what Bryn was saying we need to start talking to the werewolves. Did you hear what she said about the team losing all the time and then all of a sudden their season turns around? Considering some of the boys are now wearing cursed rings, I'm thinking that's not a coincidence."

Flora tapped on the steering wheel. "I did hear rumors that Coach Weber's job was on the line last year. Members of the school board were getting impatient with the lack of success on the field."

"Are we thinking that he could have been using some form of magic to help the boys win?" I don't know why I was surprised.

Flora winced at the suggestion. "Normal magical enhancements are screened for in the same way performance-enhancing drugs are."

"But?" I could tell from her tone there was a but.

"Magic is limitless. It's inevitable that some would not be detectable."

Of course, they wouldn't. "So, what do you suggest?" This situation had political landmine written all over it. There was no way I was walking into the middle of it.

"We can't talk to the coach. We start accusing a werewolf of consorting with witches to manipulate teenage members of the clan and Aidan will lose his mind."

I could see Flora's point. "We could go to the police," I suggested.

"You seem to be forgetting that the sheriff is away, and his position is currently being filled by an uneasy alliance between Deputy Iversen and Detective Hanlon," replied Flora. "Informing the good detective would be like handing the whole situation over to the werewolf alpha who would bury the evidence so deep we'd never get any answers."

She had a point. The last time Detective Brigitte Hanlon had run an investigation into werewolves, evidence had been mysteriously corrupted and a murderer had almost gone free.

"We do seem to have another law enforcement option

available to us." Flora's voice trailed off as if she was suggesting something unpalatable.

From my point of view, she was. "You're suggesting reporting this situation to the magisters and requesting they investigate."

She nodded. "If it looked like a witch investigation, rather than targeting werewolves, that would go some way to blunt Aidan's anger and possibly his interference."

I dropped my head at the enormity of what she was suggesting. "I'm assuming you know about Julian moving in next door to me."

"Yes," Flora replied. "I was going to talk to you about it, but the day seems to have spun out of control." She looked over at me. "My understanding is he's determined to convince you to repudiate the Destined Beloved prophecy and resume your relationship with him."

I scrubbed my hands over my face. "That pretty much covers it."

"That could be problematic."

And there was the understatement of the day. "I'm really not fond of this plan."

Flora sighed. "I don't think much of it either, but I'm struggling to come up with a better one."

The fact that I was standing on Magister Julian Bernauer's front door, ready to ask him for help, just went to prove how complicated my life had become since I moved to Walker Bay. Sure, Flora as coven leader was going to be the one to make the request, but we both knew that it was my presence that was going to make this situation interesting. I held my breath as the door opened. I don't think I'd ever seen Julian smile as brightly as he did when he found me on his front doorstep. That smile only dimmed slightly when he noticed that my aunt was accompanying me.

Before he could speak, I held up my hand. "We're here on official magister business. We have a problem."

He opened the door wide. "You are always welcome."

I motioned Flora through the door first. We had already discussed that she would be taking the lead with this situation. As we walked through the house I couldn't help looking around. When Julian and I had been going out together, we'd mostly spent time at my home. I frowned as I realized this was the first time I had ever seen where Julian lived. That really should have been a clue.

Julian indicated a couch for us to sit on and he took a chair opposite.

"Now, how can the Conclave be of service to the Walker Bay Coven?"

I looked on quietly as Flora explained our censored version of the situation. I couldn't help the feeling of being exposed as Flora told Julian about Lisa and her lesions, and the aggression in members of the football team. At this stage we were keeping quiet about Bryn's nose shrinking cream and the fact that these were curses and not prank spells that had got out of hand. We were hoping that the effects of the curses were so far below the traditional expectation of what a curse should be that nobody would suspect.

When Flora finished, she smiled at Julian expectantly. "As you can understand, approaching the alpha about inter-viewing werewolves is a delicate matter, especially as we are concerned that they may be messing with witchcraft. We were hoping that if you were to instigate the investigation, there would be fewer political issues."

Julian leaned back in his chair. "I'm surprised you haven't called the sheriff in on this one. Surely this would be his jurisdiction."

I lifted my head. "We are currently not in contact with the sheriff. As far as I am aware, he has only spoken to his brother. As Eamon is the eldest son of the werewolf alpha, you can understand why we would be reluctant to ask his assistance."

Julian's eyes gleamed at the information I had just relayed. If the situation wasn't quite so important, I would have been tempted to kick him.

"Any spells, even if they're just pranks, being cast on werewolves is always a cause for concern. If the football team has been magically dosed, that means there is something getting through our testing procedures. That can't be allowed to continue." He slapped his hands down on his knees. "You were right to bring this to me. Rogue witches who practice unauthorized magic need to be stamped out. There is no room for those kinds of people in a civilized society."

A chill ran through me at Julian's words. Deep down, I knew that I was one of those people that he believed needed to be removed from civilized society. I could feel my heart racing at the enormity of my position. I was sitting in the house, asking for help from the man who could very well cause my downfall. I looked at Flora and hoped she was finished. Once we'd put this situation in the hands of the magisters, I was going to go back to my library and days of boredom with the hermit.

"Of course, I'm going to need Sadie's assistance."

I coughed as my fear gripped me around the throat. "Why? I don't know any of these people and none of them respect me. I'm seen as a null in this town. The only reason I'm tolerated is because of Flora and the Destined Beloved prophecy. If it wasn't for those two things I would probably have been banished to the Glen."

I may have been exaggerating there a little. I didn't really think I'd be banished to the Glen with all the other outcasts, but I was trying to make a point. That point being that the last thing I wanted to do was to spend time with the one man I should stay as far away from as possible.

"Regardless, I want you working with me."

"Sadie has other responsibilities. We need her in the coven library, and she is my apprentice. My need is greater," Flora hissed, her normal serenity ruffled by the way this situation had turned.

"Oh, I doubt that very much," drawled Julian.

"Why?" I asked, fighting to keep the panic out of my voice. "I'm no use to an investigation. You have to know that."

"Two reasons," stated Julian. "The first reason is because I want to spend time with you. Stubborn as you are, you would never agree to that normally. This situation means you need me. We're skating on the edge of jurisdiction on this one and I'm going to have to argue with the Conclave to get them to approve me stepping on werewolf toes. I should get something out of that, and the only thing I want is to spend time with Sadie."

Yep, I really wanted to kick him. I glanced at Flora and saw she was battling the same inclination.

"Second, Collette Harstone has been informed that she has a granddaughter who is living in Walker Bay and is apprenticed to her sister."

I knew it was unreasonable to expect that my presence in Walker Bay would go unnoticed, but I had hoped.

I felt Flora stiffen beside me. "Collette has no claim on Sadie."

"No, she doesn't," Julian said gently, "but she is curious about this unknown grandchild. She has chosen to step back and allow Sadie to find her powers before claiming her for the Harstone family."

"Translation is that she doesn't want to sully the Harstone name with a null," I said roughly, grateful that Doran and Bryn had reminded me of that charming term. My eyes narrowed as an ugly suspicion wormed its way through my mind. "If you've been sent to spy on me and report back to her, you can give her this message. I'm a Goodwin, not a Harstone. I don't care if I come into my powers or not, that fact is never going to change. I am really not interested in playing happy families with anybody else."

Julian leaned forward. "I'm not here to spy on you. My

job was initially to watch for signs of more rogue witches. The incidents the last few months have caused some consternation. When she found out I was coming back here, Collette approached me as she was concerned that you had ended up in Walker Bay without the steadying influence of your family." He grimaced as he glanced over at Flora. "Her words, not mine." He swung his focus back to me. "She asked me to watch over you, make sure you were safe. I swear, that was all I intended to do. I need you to believe that I would never betray you."

I wished I could believe that, but I had a bad feeling that the day was coming soon when he would be forced to do just that.

I couldn't help being subdued as we left Julian's house with a promise that he would speak to the Conclave about starting an investigation. Until then, we would have to wait. Flora and I didn't say a word to each other until we were safely in my house and I had activated my troll doll. Since discovering that a magister had tried to hack into it and failed, I now didn't trust anything else to protect my private conversations.

"You're going to need to be careful," Flora said, finally breaking through the silence. "As far as the Conclave is concerned, you are a null. Do not do anything that would change that opinion."

I didn't plan to. I put my hands over my face and took a couple of deep breaths. When I was feeling calm, I stood up straight. "I'll be fine. I'm just feeling a little overwhelmed. When I woke up this morning, I did not expect this to happen."

Flora put a sympathetic hand on my arm. "I wish I could protect you from this."

"Which part?" I laughed humorlessly. "The part where I'm blackmailed into spending time with my ex-boyfriend for an investigation I want to be as far from as I could possibly get, or maybe where I find out he's watching me for my absent grandmother. He didn't even mention Jasper. Do you think my father knows about me?"

I really didn't like the note of wistfulness I heard in my voice. I was going to have to squash that hope before it got me hurt. Considering what I knew about Jasper's character, it most definitely would.

"You need to go see Arthur."

My head snapped up at the random comment from Flora. "I don't have time to sit and listen to that man drone on about things that have no relevance to what is happening here and now."

I had to go back to work. As the librarian for the coven library I had access to a bank of knowledge that was incredible. I may have to be careful about my contribution to the investigation while I was working with Julian, but I could gather all the information that I could find and pass it to Flora.

"You need to see Arthur," Flora repeated. She grabbed my hands to stop the incessant waving I seemed to be doing. "Trust me. He will be able to help you."

I could see the desperation in her eyes. This woman had given me a home, a family and a purpose.

"Fine," I said. "I'll go see him."

As I stood outside the door of Arthur McClune's cabin, I was slightly annoyed at how quickly I caved.

"I wasn't sure you would come back, Goodwin."

I turned around. I didn't understand why the man had a house. He never seemed to be in it.

"Flora insists that you can help me."

McClune watched me shrewdly. "You don't agree with her."

"I think your knowledge has its place," I said carefully. "And if I had the time, I would relish learning about the full and rich history of a world that I've only caught a glimpse of."

"But you don't have the time," he replied.

"There's just so much of it and the last time we barely got started. I need to know things that are affecting me now."

McClune crossed his arms and waited.

Encouraged by the lack of argument from him I sat down on the porch. "I need to know more about why werewolves and witches hate each other so much and how the Conclave got so powerful. I need to know why Seers are considered infallible and whether they have ever been wrong. I also need to know how football works in paranormal towns."

I know, the football thing was a bit random but the more I considered it, the more I wondered how it didn't become a bloodbath. I mean, think about it. You have a field filled with werewolves, witches, ogres, centaurs, and who knows what other paranormal beings. I defy anyone to picture that scene and not have it devolve into absolute carnage.

"You're asking me about football?"

I could tell from the raised eyebrow that I had managed to surprise him. I took a chance that he was as trustworthy and knowledgeable as Flora believed.

"It seems the kids in the football team have been acting with some unexplained aggression lately. There is some concern that witchcraft could be involved in their championship win."

McClune's lip curled in a sneer. "I wouldn't be surprised with Doug Weber as the coach."

"You know him?"

"Like your father, he was an unpleasant child. From what I recall, they were friends, of a fashion."

I knew he was waiting for a reaction, so I kept my expression blank.

"He has always been somebody who needed to win at any cost. He always had to have the best career, the best family, the best life." The smile McClune gave was not a pleasant one. "As so often happens with people like that, they fall far short of the image they project."

"In what way?" I asked, keeping my voice quiet.

"When he was in high school there were rumors that his talents on the football field were not entirely natural."

"You mean he was taking drugs?"

McClune shrugged. "There are many ways to enhance the performance of a player. Some from your world, some from ours. Drugs were definitely an option available to an aspiring athlete, determined to be the best at any cost. If a werewolf was ambitious enough and had the right connections, there are witches who are willing to provide potions or spells for the right price. Some of these are detectable. The best of them aren't. All of them have consequences."

I mulled over his words. "Were there any witches he was particularly friendly with at that time?"

McClune tilted his head as if thinking hard, the sun shining through the silver of his hair and beard. "Your father was long gone by the time Weber hit high school or I would have suggested him. He would definitely be the type to engage in those kinds of illicit activities."

I rolled my eyes. "I get it. You didn't like Jasper Harstone. At no time am I going to defend him, so you need to move on. He was nine years old when he left town so we can be relatively sure he had nothing to do with this. Let's focus on the here and now."

I was surprised to hear the old man chuckle, although it had a rusty quality to it.

"That must have hurt," I commented. "You seem to be the kind of person who doesn't find much joy in the world."

McClune instantly sobered. "The joy was stolen out of my life a long time ago."

I wasn't given much time to consider his words as he became all business again.

"I don't know of any witches in his teenage years, but I have it on reliable authority that Coach Weber has not been keeping faithful to his wedding vows, and his dalliances of choice are with witches."

And there we were. What was it with werewolves and the forbidden?

"Was there any witch in particular?" I asked. "Or is he doing the werewolf thing and sharing the love?"

"Weber is smarter than he looks. He doesn't indulge his vice in Walker Bay. Too many chances of him getting caught by somebody who knows his wife. He prefers to stick with transients, witches who are only around for a very short period of time."

"Like Travelers," I murmured, not liking the picture I was seeing.

"Travelers would fit the bill perfectly. Their magic sometimes pushes the boundaries of what the Conclave feels is acceptable. A man like Weber would be drawn to someone like that." He paused. "If ever you get the opportunity to question him, you might want to ask him about the Albatross Inn down the coast. My understanding is it is his preferred rendezvous point."

Flora was right. Arthur McClune was full of information.

He clapped his hands together. "Enough about unpleasant members of our community. You've come here to learn. We will continue from where we left off yesterday."

Inwardly I groaned. I should have known things were going too well.

13

*B*efore I tackled what I was sure was going to be an unpleasant day, I took ten minutes to greet the morning on my deck. I wanted to give myself the opportunity to find some peace. You would think by now that I would realize that was never going to happen.

"Are you out of your ever-loving mind?"

I should have expected that Tilda would have heard about the arrangement with Julian. If I didn't know that her magical ability was herbal lore, I would have assumed it was telepathy. She seemed to be tapped into a greater consciousness and knew gossip as soon as it happened.

"Liam?" I guessed and wasn't surprised when she nodded. She also seemed to have the ability to get information out of the magister with surprising ease, although I wasn't entirely sure whether that talent could be defined as magical.

I watched as Tilda tried to visibly calm her anger. "I can't believe you would be such an idiot."

I guess that was as close to calm as we were going to get.

"I wasn't really given much of a choice."

Understanding dawned on Tilda. "He's holding something over you."

I shrugged. "Let's just say that if I want something done, I have to play by his rules."

Having negotiated my precarious deck Tilda slid down next to me. "Seriously, what is it with men?" I could see the concern in her eyes. "Are you going to be okay with this?"

"Why wouldn't I be okay? The man who is supposed to be here to do this job has cut all contact with me, and the one who I was sure I would never see again is living next to me and seems to want to spend every waking moment with me." I dropped my head. "Why is this all so difficult?"

"Are you ever sorry that you got dragged into this?"

I looked up to see guilt and concern on Tilda's face, although considering it was her grandmother who was actually the one who kidnapped me, I had no idea why Tilda felt guilty.

"I'm happy to be here," I said quietly as I took in the view. "I'm just having trouble working out how my life became so complicated." I took in a deep breath. "I blame Maude."

Tilda gave a short laugh. "That's usually a safe way to go." She sobered. "Speaking of she who must be obeyed, Grandma's on her way home."

I frowned at that piece of news. "I thought she was going to be away for a few more weeks."

Tilda sighed. "That was the plan, but when she found out about Lisa, she cut her trip short because there is no way I could handle this situation without her input." You could almost see the sarcasm dripping from every word.

I was about to answer her when a new voice entered the conversation. "Are you ready to start our day?"

I was really going to have to get Flora to put up wards so not just anybody could come up to this deck. It was becoming busier than the diner.

"I thought I was going to come by your place and we would get started then," I said through gritted teeth.

Julian gave me a blinding smile. "I received the go-ahead from the Conclave and figured you would want to get started straight away, seeing as you brought the situation to me." He sobered as his gaze moved to Tilda. "How is your sister recovering from her ordeal?"

"She is fine," Tilda replied as she stood and proceeded to haul me up as well.

She gave me a hug and whispered words of encouragement which may or may not have included threats of bodily damage to the magister if he dared to put a foot wrong. She then proceeded to leave me alone with the last man I wanted to be alone with. If there had been slightly more loathing in the glare she gave him, I was pretty sure it would have been capable of physically damaging him.

"She doesn't like me very much, does she?" Julian asked as he watched Tilda carefully make her way down the stairs.

"She's a loyal friend," I told him. "Liam is very lucky to have caught her attention."

Julian sighed. "So he keeps saying." He focused his attention back on me. "I'm assuming you're not ready yet."

I looked down at my flannel pajamas with the cat pattern which had seemed so cute when I'd bought it. "I can see why you're the magister. You've got some keen powers of observation there."

Julian chuckled. "Hurry up and get ready. We are meeting the rest of the team at the diner in twenty minutes."

I froze as the implication of what he was saying got through. "The rest of the team," I croaked. "As in Liam and your fiancée?"

Julian grimaced. "Ex-fiancée. I told you that I'd broken the arranged betrothal. Anyway, she's a magister of the

Conclave. There is no way she would allow a personal situation to interfere with her professional responsibilities."

I could not help the dumbfounded expression that I knew was on my face. It amazed me that such an intelligent man could be such an idiot.

14

From the moment I walked into the diner, with Julian's hand inappropriately resting on my lower back, I could tell that Penelope Hartford was not okay with the fact that Julian had broken off their arranged betrothal. I wasn't sure whether she'd actually had any feelings for him or whether her pride had taken a hit, but she was seething with anger, and it was all directed at me. I sat down next to Liam thinking that his relationship with my best friend made him the closest thing to an ally I had at this table. I still couldn't believe this situation had got so out of control. When Flora and I had first discussed bringing the magisters in on this investigation, it had been with the clear understanding that we would dump the whole werewolf mess in their laps, make an ordered retreat, and clean up any curse related issues in a discreet fashion on the periphery. What was happening now was very far from that plan.

"Good to see you're part of the team." There was encouragement in Liam's voice, but I could see the strain around his eyes. It looked like he had the same concerns about this plan as I did.

Hartford didn't even try to hide her displeasure, but she seemed to have more discipline than to make her irritation known. I was sure that was going to happen later. "What are we doing?"

"There is some concern that there has been magical juicing of the local football team. Members have been showing abnormal aggression levels."

"How can you tell the difference?" muttered Liam. "That's their natural state."

"It hasn't just been the werewolves," Julian replied sternly. "At least one of the witch members of the team seem to also be affected, and there has also been a case of a prank spell that seems to have got out of hand."

"Lovely town you have here," Hartford bit out in her first recognition that I was at the table.

I shrugged. "Teenagers." I figured using that response had worked as an answer for my mother so many times that I may as well use it myself.

Hartford did not look impressed.

"The Conclave has been in contact with the alpha who has agreed, albeit reluctantly, to allow us to interview werewolf members of the team and coaching staff." Julian cleared his throat. "There was one concession we had to make."

My head snapped up at that statement. So far, this investigation had been about backroom deals and personal interests. I hated to think what Aidan Tolan had brought to the table.

"His eldest son, Eamon, will be joining us."

Okay, compared to the other surprises I'd had this week, that wasn't the worst. I glanced over at Liam who still had that strained look around his eyes. This was not going to be a good time for him. Liam might not know that Eamon hated him purely for the fact that he was dating Tilda, but as the victim of choice for werewolf disapproval in Walker Bay, I knew how it felt to have waves of dislike beating down on you. I took a moment to feel sympathy for the magister. On the other hand, a test of his determination to be with Tilda might not go astray.

"We will be joining Tolan at the town meeting hall where he has gathered all the players in the clan." Julian narrowed his eyes at his two teammates. "I expect complete professionalism when dealing with the werewolf."

It concerned me that he actually had to say that.

WHEN WE ARRIVED at the town hall, I expected to find more sullen teenagers. Instead, we found a simmering pot of testosterone just waiting for that one spark to make it explode. I could tell Eamon was at the end of his rope when he grabbed the shoulder of one of the boys who had started coming out of his chair at the sight of us and shoved him back down.

"You can't make me talk to them," spat the boy.

"Thank you for volunteering, Benton. For attempting to defy your alpha's wishes, you are going first," Eamon growled.

I recognized him now. Benton Westcotte was one of the boys who had started fighting in the diner. A glance at his finger confirmed the presence of the ring and the tendrils coiled around it. I searched the hall to find Aaron Pixton. Unlike the other boys who looked like they were ready to launch themselves into battle, Aaron was nervous, looking around with a wide-eyed stare as if he couldn't believe what he was seeing. I checked his hand and found he didn't have a ring. That explained whose ring I had ended up destroying. Eamon dragged Benton into a side office so we could talk to him in private. I know Julian hoped that this would make him more willing to talk if he was separated from his friends. I had a feeling the presence of the ring would make all normal tactics useless.

Julian settled in a chair opposite Benton and the rest of us spread ourselves around the room. Eamon moved close to me and I could tell that he was confused by my presence. I wish I could explain but I didn't think I could come up with any explanation that didn't send up warning flags.

Julian smiled at the boy and I knew he was trying to appear friendly. I also knew it wasn't going to make one bit of difference. That curse had Benton tightly within its grasp. I had to exercise all my self-control to prevent myself from lurching forward and ripping that ring from his hand and destroying it.

"We have reason to believe that you boys have been using enhancing magic to improve your performance on the football field," Julian started, his voice calm and measured. "We don't blame you," he emphasized. "We think some adults in your life took advantage of your determination to win and we need you to tell us who they were." He caught Benton's eye. "Any assistance you give would be greatly appreciated by the Conclave and it will go some way to mitigating your own guilt in this situation."

Benton leaned forward. "You think I'm going to tell a filthy witch anything? I don't answer to you. I don't answer to anyone."

Before Julian could respond, I heard Eamon growl. "You answer to the hierarchy. You answer to your alpha."

I didn't like the manic look that settled in Benton's eyes. "Maybe it's time for a new hierarchy and a new alpha."

Eamon was a blur as he yanked Benton out of his chair and immediately had him pressed to the ground. I could feel the oppression of Eamon's dominance power and Benton started whimpering as if in pain. I looked around and saw each of the magisters was having trouble controlling their response to Eamon's power. I was surprised at his strength. I had thought only the alpha could be that strong. I had a flash of fear go through me as I wondered if Aidan realized how strong his son was. Based on what I knew about Aidan and his desperate need to assert himself as the strongest werewolf, I really hoped not.

"I would suggest you rethink some of your ideas, pup. My father is nowhere close to being as patient as I am. Spout that nonsense anywhere within his hearing and you will feel the full wrath of the alpha."

He let go of the boy who was now a quivering mess on the floor. I looked around at the magisters and their reaction to Eamon's power. Each of them had an expression of varying degrees of contempt and distaste. In that moment I was glad I'd been raised far away from this world and its prejudices. I liked the fact that I could see the man Eamon was, untainted by centuries of animosity.

"We're done with this one," Eamon snarled as he grabbed hold of Benton's collar. He dragged the terrified boy out.

"I hate dealing with werewolves," Hartford muttered. "They're so barbaric."

Considering some of the atrocities I had seen committed by witches since I had come to Walker Bay, I was struck by the hypocrisy of her statement.

"Quiet," snapped Julian. "We have been afforded a privilege by the werewolves. Do not seek to abuse it."

I wondered how much of that statement was a strongly held belief, and how much was the knowledge that werewolf hearing meant we could be overheard. I didn't have any time to think through that question as Eamon led Aaron into the office, his face giving no indication that he had heard the exchange.

Unlike Benton, Aaron looked scared and very confused. I

could see that Julian saw the difference in this boy. In a belated attempt to soothe Aaron's nerves he brought out what I recognized to be a privacy stone.

"You know what this is, don't you?"

Aaron nodded.

Julian gave an encouraging smile. "So you know that whatever you say will not be overheard by anybody outside of this room."

Aaron nodded again.

"Can you explain what has been happening with you and your friends?" Julian asked, keeping his tone low and gentle.

"I don't know." Aaron frowned. "Yesterday, I just started feeling so angry with everything and everybody. I just wanted to hurt someone. I didn't care who."

"And it only started yesterday?" I interjected.

Julian looked annoyed at my interruption, but as far as I was concerned, he dragged me along for this ride. He could deal with the consequences of that decision.

"Yes," Aaron replied.

I frowned at what he was saying. The boys had got the championship rings at the end of last season which had been months ago. I didn't understand why they would only start feeling the effects of the curse within the last twenty-four hours.

Julian took back control of the interview. "Have you boys been using any enhancements for your football?"

For the first time Aaron lost the defeated look on his face. "Definitely not. We would never do anything like that. We won the season, fair and square."

I searched his face for any deception, and I couldn't find any.

"Thank you," Julian said smoothly. "If you think of anything else, please contact me."

I don't know why he wasted his time. These kids were

here under duress. If they had information they would be going to Eamon, and if we were very lucky, he would share it with us.

When the two werewolves left Julian turned to me, his irritation obvious. "This is my investigation," he bit out. "I ask the questions."

I widened my eyes at Julian's harsh tone. "If you want me to leave, I'm happy to go. You were the one who dragged me into this, remember." I was pretty sure we weren't going to get any more coherent answers than the ones Aaron had given us. I was happy to walk.

"You stay," Julian replied. "Just remember who's in charge."

I wasn't likely to forget.

After Aaron, teenager after teenager came through that room, and all of them gave us nothing. They spat out obscenities, abused our parentage, and a couple of them even tried to launch themselves out of their chairs and attack us, but not one of them gave us anything close to resembling an answer to our questions. After the last one, I blew out an impatient breath. That had been a complete waste of time.

Eamon came back in the room. "I've just received word that the coach and his assistant are ready to be interviewed. We need to go to Coach Weber's house."

Julian frowned. "Why can't he come here?"

Eamon gave him a withering look. "You magisters really need to work on your knowledge of werewolves. I was able to get the team together because they are kids and their level on the hierarchy is not set. We are not so fortunate with Coach Weber. The only reason he is talking to you is because the alpha requested it."

I had to stop myself from snorting out loud. Aidan Tolan was not the sort of alpha who made requests. I had a feeling Doug Weber wasn't given much of a choice.

"Very well," Julian replied, his irritation evident.

"And Sadie will be coming with me."

I had to admit I was surprised by Eamon's demand.

"No." Julian's reply was short and to the point.

"Her Destined Beloved is my brother. That makes her family. That means it is my job to protect her from anything or anyone I perceive as a threat."

It didn't take a genius to work out Eamon's meaning. Although, considering one member of the Tolan family had tried to kill me and most of the others hated me on sight, I couldn't say I was overly thrilled at Eamon's effort to claim me.

It didn't take a genius to see that Julian wasn't pleased with that plan. Apparently, Eamon picked up on that too.

"Let me put this another way. Sadie comes with me or all access to the werewolf clan is revoked."

And there was that Tolan arrogance that I was becoming so familiar with. I can't say that I had missed it.

15

*T*he second we got in Eamon's truck I activated the troll doll. The last thing I wanted was for Julian to try to listen in on this conversation, and I had no doubt he would.

"Did you want to explain to me what's going on?" Despite his calm tone I could tell that Eamon wasn't coping well with the situation. "Last night my father informs me that he is doing a favor for the Conclave, he wants me to work with magisters to investigate werewolves, and now I find you're spending time with your ex-boyfriend. I'm currently debating which of those situations is causing me the most concern.

I could see his dilemma. "What do you think our chances would have been if Flora and I had gone to Aidan, and asked him if we could interview werewolf members of the football team and coaching staff about using performance-enhancing magic to win the championship last season?"

Eamon grimaced at what was obviously an unpleasant image. "I would say not great."

"That's what we figured. We've been finding some

unusual spells and we're concerned we might have a rogue witch who is messing with the teenagers in this town. After what I saw in the diner yesterday, I'm concerned the football team may be involved. With the sheriff gone we turned to our best chance of finding out what's going on. Unfortunately, for witches that means the magisters."

Eamon went silent as he contemplated my explanation. "It still doesn't explain why you're working with the magisters.

I decided to go for honesty. "Julian refused to make the request of the Conclave unless I was involved."

Eamon groaned. "I thought he'd accepted the Destined Beloved prophecy."

"Apparently not."

"Conall is going to lose his mind. What did you tell him?"

I stared straight ahead. "I haven't heard from your brother since the day he left Walker Bay."

Eamon swore under his breath. "He's an idiot."

If Eamon was expecting me to disagree with him, he was going to be sorely disappointed.

After some silence Eamon's shoulders slumped. "How do you suggest I deal with this?"

I glanced over at him. "You should go along with the investigation. Something bad is happening and if we don't get to the bottom of it, I have a feeling it is going to get worse. Despite the fact none of us are keen on them being involved, if there is a rogue witch causing harm to these kids, the magisters are our best allies in catching them."

Eamon grunted in displeasure.

I took a deep breath and decided to take a chance. "I would also suggest that you very discreetly gather the championship rings from each of those boys and bring them to me tonight. Do not say anything to the magisters about it. Flora and I believe there is something magical about them that is causing the majority of the problems in their behavior. We also believe that if the magisters get involved with that part of the investigation, the situation could become problematic."

"I need more than that," Eamon growled.

Despite my fondness for Eamon, I wasn't willing to give him more. "I am giving you an option. I don't know if it will solve all your problems, but it may help." I took in a breath. "Your brother trusts me. I would hope you would too."

I could see Eamon struggling. Not having complete control over the situation was not something he coped well with. His shoulders slumped at the point that he realized he had no other options.

"Fine, I'll get the rings from the boys. Is there anything else?"

I thought for a moment. "Is there any chance Flora and I can talk to Cleo Moore, separate to the magisters?"

Eamon raised an eyebrow as if waiting for an explanation. When none was forthcoming, he sighed. "I'll see what I can do."

I patted him on the arm. "With any luck this will be cleared up quickly, the magisters will realize we don't need them here and we can go back to being a peaceful, quiet town." Despite not ever seeing that side of Walker Bay, I had been assured that it used to be that way. Before I arrived. I hoped that was just a coincidence.

"Looking forward to that day," growled Eamon.

WE MET the magisters at Doug Weber's house, and from the irritated expression on Julian's face I was guessing that he had been trying to listen in on the conversation I had with

Eamon and had failed. This was confirmed when he pulled me to one side.

"What did you tell him?" Julian hissed.

Despite reminding myself that as a cursebreaker I had the ability to lie with impunity and a magister would read it as the truth, I decided to stick with a relatively accurate account of our conversation.

"I told him that Flora and I went through the Conclave because we didn't believe the alpha would entertain our request to speak to the kids. I also explained the reason I am here with you."

"That's it?"

I smiled and answered with the confidence of somebody who was learning that the ability to lie to law enforcement was a valuable gift to have. "Yes, that is all we talked about. That and how angry the sheriff is going to be when he finds out."

"Then he shouldn't have left you, should he?" Julian bit out.

I visibly flinched at the direct hit and Julian must have thought better of it.

"I'm sorry, that was uncalled for."

It didn't make it any less true. I straightened and stepped back from Julian. "We need to get this done."

I started walking towards the house, and I could see from the anger on Eamon's face that he had overheard everything that was said. I shook my head slightly, hoping that he wouldn't decide to take his recently self-declared status as family member seriously.

DOUG WEBER WAS EXACTLY what I thought a werewolf football coach would be. Big, brash and full of confidence in himself and his place in the community. To say he was annoyed at our presence was an understatement. Nothing short of a direct order from his alpha was going to convince this man to talk to us, and he intended to do it as reluctantly and insolently as possible. If it wasn't so important for us to get the information, I would have enjoyed the way the coach was sparring with Julian.

"You are saying that the amazing turn around that we saw in your team was purely due to hard work and dedication?"

Julian's condescending tone was rubbing both Coach Weber and the assistant coach, Peter Martel, the wrong way. To be fair, if he'd spoken to me like that, I would have been tempted to cause him some bodily damage too.

"The kids found their heart and put their head in the game. I couldn't be prouder of the way they fought back."

If I didn't know better, I would have thought I was in a post-game press conference.

Julian gave a smile that didn't reach his eyes. "Are you sure that there wasn't any temptation to enhance their performances in other ways? Drugs, perhaps?"

The assistant coach, who until this moment had let the coach do all the talking, decided to add to the conversation. "All our boys are rigorously drug tested. There is no chance any of them are taking drugs."

I wondered whether the man was lying or deluded. From the look on Julian's face I could tell he agreed with me.

"Athletes have been getting away with taking performance-enhancing drugs for decades without getting caught. What makes you so sure that your team is any different?"

Despite his obvious annoyance with the magister, Martel kept his voice even. "It wasn't just one or two of the boys that improved. Every single kid on that team stepped up. The only way that could happen if drugs were involved is if every one of the boys was taking them. That wouldn't happen. We have a mixed team of races here. We can barely get them all to agree to train at the same time. For them all to suddenly start taking drugs would be impossible."

"Unless they were doped unwillingly."

There was a swift intake of breath at Julian's words and Eamon stepped forward.

"You're crossing the line," he growled.

"Nobody on my staff would dope our kids," Weber snarled, looking as if he was a hairsbreadth away from turning into a wolf and ripping Julian apart. "And there is no way we could do that without the kids' knowledge which brings us back to the non-werewolf players who aren't likely to just go along with a program like that."

Julian held up his hands but there was no surrendering in this encounter. "What about magic enhancements? That could be done without the players being aware. Somebody collects talismans from each of the boys - a bit of hair here, a sweaty shirt there - and you have everything you need for a spell that will mean the coaching staff doesn't get fired at the end of another losing season."

I winced at the direct shot at the coach's pride. It looked like Julian had decided to play hardball.

Weber lurched to his feet. "I would never have anything to do with a filthy witch."

Even though I knew this was the last thing I should do, the opening was too good.

"Are you sure? Because my understanding is that you enjoy getting a room at the Albatross Inn with any Traveler witch who catches your eye."

There was a full three seconds of silence as every stunned eye in the room turned to me. Eamon, knowing how a married werewolf who cared about his place in the hierarchy would react to that kind of accusation, was the first to move and he pulled me into his side. Weber was reaching for me when I started to feel a pressure that I had learned to equate to the dominance power that certain members of the community were able to wield. I was shocked when everybody else in the room dropped to their knees. I thought only an alpha would be able to dominate magisters, and even then it wasn't a guarantee. It seemed Eamon was stronger than anyone believed. I could see Julian was down on one knee, fighting the power that couldn't be seen. He was the closest to being able to rise but it was like a boulder was placed on his shoulders that he was straining against. Hartford and Liam were prone on the floor, desperately trying to fight their way to their feet, but failing. Both Weber and Martel weren't even trying. A lifetime in the werewolf hierarchy had taught them to submit.

"We are done here," Eamon snarled. "I am revoking the Conclave's access to any werewolves of the clan." He pointed to Weber and I could feel him push a little more power at the coach. "You are never to lay a hand on Sadie. She is my brother's Destined Beloved and as such is under my protection. Approach her and your life is forfeit."

Weber whimpered. I couldn't hear an answer, but Eamon must have been satisfied because he pulled back on the power and turned towards the magisters.

"I want all of you out of here."

With that he turned his back as if to dismiss us, but not before he gave me a look which told me we were going to have words the next time he saw me.

16

I followed the magisters out of the house. We were in the car when Julian turned to me.

"How did you know about the inn?" His voice was deceptively calm.

"Local knowledge," I said. "You three have been here five minutes. I live in this community and I talk to the people here, and sometimes that means coming into possession of some gossip. I'd heard Coach Weber isn't the greatest of husbands and he likes fooling around with witches, but not ones that might run into his wife. I also heard he likes the Albatross Inn up the coast to keep things discreet."

Julian nodded and stayed silent until we had dropped Hartford and Liam off at their homes. Assuming that we'd be returning to our street, I was surprised when we started heading out of town.

"Where are we going?" I asked, wondering what my survival rate would be if I flung myself out of a moving car.

"I thought we'd check out this Albatross Inn, see if anybody can give us an idea about any witches that Weber might have been seeing."

That sounded like a good idea. I settled back in my seat and enjoyed the view from the coast road.

Julian cleared his throat. "Did you want to tell me how you were able to withstand that dominance play the werewolf did?"

Not particularly, but I could see he wasn't going to let it go. "Eamon may have deliberately left me out of it," I suggested.

Julian glanced at me. "I don't think so. The kind of power he used in that situation is not very well-honed. If he had time, he may have been able to make that distinction, but everything happened too fast. You should have gone down with the rest of us. I've also been told by my team that you aren't affected by the coven leader or the werewolf alpha when they use the power."

I shrugged. "Maybe it has something to do with the Destined Beloved prophecy and Conall being a berserker. I don't know why it doesn't work on me."

I really didn't like the way Julian was watching me. I could almost see the wheels spinning in his head. I just hoped he didn't land on the correct answer.

Desperate to distract him I pointed to a building in the distance. "There it is."

Julian squinted. "How do you know?"

"I visited once when I was exploring the area. There isn't much out here except for the inn. I wouldn't have taken it for the kind of place for an illicit affair you were trying to hide."

"What would you think it would be used for?"

I shrugged. "I don't know. Couple's romantic weekend, honeymoon, something special."

"Does the berserker take you to places like that?"

"Don't," I warned. "That part of my life is off limits to you."

"You know he will never be able to understand you like

another witch would, and this case is providing a perfect example of the faithlessness of werewolves. He hasn't contacted you in two weeks. At best he's taking you for granted. At worst he is trapped by this prophecy and looking elsewhere for what he really wants."

"How can you say that?" I hissed, furious at him.

Julian kept his eyes on the road. "Because nine months ago I was him, trapped by an arranged marriage and centuries of expectations. Then one day I went for a walk in a park and met you. For the first time in my life I was torn between my duty and what I wanted. I had to make a choice and I did what was expected. I left you and returned to my family and the destiny that was laid out for me."

I stayed silent. There was nowhere to go, and Julian obviously needed to get this out.

"But it wasn't enough. I may have gone back but I grew resentful of the arrangement and my family. All I wanted was to return to you." As we pulled up at the front of the inn Julian turned to me. "He will come back because his duty will demand it, but you can never be sure that he doesn't resent you for the trap he finds himself in."

I turned back to the man I had once loved. "I don't know what will happen with this prophecy, but I do know if you don't stop trying to convince me to put it aside, I will begin to hate you."

Julian took a breath. "Very well, those will be my last words on the matter. Just know, I will be waiting for you when the prophecy proves false."

He got out of the car and headed towards the inn. It took me a little longer to calm down before I followed him. By the time I caught up to him, Julian was already talking to the woman behind the desk who seemed smitten by the handsome magister. In his hand he had created what looked like a holographic image of Coach Weber. I was slightly surprised by the sight. It was weird sometimes to remember that Julian was a witch. He didn't seem to go out of his way to show off his powers, so that made the times I saw them so much more striking. The image Julian conjured was a good one. Although he must have done it from his own interpreted memory as it seemed to have a vicious sneer to it.

"You're sure you've never seen this gentleman here?"

The young woman shook her head and I had a thought.

"Do you have any accommodation where the room has an external door so the guest can enter it without going through this main area?"

The woman's eyes brightened. "You mean the Garden Room. It has glass doors which open out onto the garden and you can walk down to the ocean."

That sounded about right. "Could we have a quick look at it?"

She looked around and then peered at Julian. "Usually we shouldn't, but since you're a magister, I think it would be okay."

She reached behind the desk and passed Julian the key. "Go down the hallway and it's the last room on your right."

Julian nodded. "Thank you for your assistance. We will get this back to you soon."

"What made you think of that?" Julian asked as we made our way down the hall.

"Everything I heard about Coach Weber indicates he was trying very hard to hide this predilection of his from both his wife and the rest of the town. He isn't going to stroll up to the front desk and check in. He's going to get the woman of the hour to do the paperwork, pay for the room, and then he will join her, out of sight of everybody. That way there is no chance of anybody ever knowing what he is doing."

"But you did know." Julian's eyes narrowed. "Tell me again how you knew."

"Like I said, I've found out things over the last few months and I'm not going to betray anybody's trust by ratting them out to a magister."

After a few seconds Julian replied. "Fair enough."

When we got to the room Julian opened the door and we stepped inside.

"This is lovely," I breathed as I took in the stunning view through the garden and out over the ocean. "Why would somebody waste this room on a seedy affair. You should share this room with somebody you actually care about."

"Yes, you should," murmured Julian.

The tension in the room rose and I cleared my throat. "So, what do we do now? We've got a theory, but we have no way of knowing whether it's right or who Coach Weber was meeting, unless you have a forensics kit that can collect DNA or fingerprints."

Julian chuckled. "Sometimes I forget how new you are to this world. Just stand back and watch."

He stood in the center of the room and held his hands out. He started using a language that I was not yet familiar with. I watched as shapes of light started to coalesce into the vague outlines of people who moved around the room as if we weren't there. I couldn't hear what they were saying, and I could barely tell what they were doing. It was like I was watching a very old and faded movie. I frowned as I realized that the people were going in reverse.

"This is how we'll find out whether Coach Weber was here."

While I'd been fascinated by the images, Julian had stepped out of the center of the room and was standing next to me.

"How did you do that?"

Julian smiled sheepishly. "This is my innate ability. I can bring the past back to life...kind of..."

"Wow," I breathed. "That must be so fascinating. Can you go to historical sites and do that?"

Julian nodded. "The older the site, the more exhausted I become, but it is worth it to watch history unfold."

My eyes shone as I thought of what he could see. "That's amazing, I would love power like that." I tilted my head as an image took shape. "What are they...?" I slapped my hands over my eyes. "They're having sex."

Julian laughed out loud. "I'd forgotten how prudish you are. What did you expect we would see? It's a hotel room."

I kept one hand over my eyes and waved the other in front of me. "I didn't expect that. Don't you have a way of censoring it?"

"I can speed it up until we find Weber. Is that good enough?"

"Sure, because watching porn at super speed is exactly how I wanted to spend my day."

Julian continued to chuckle as I stood in the corner of the room, trying desperately to look anywhere but where the action was.

"Here we are," Julian said as he slowed down the images and started moving them forward.

Despite the now obvious downside, I still had to admit this power was right up there with Maude's elemental ability as my favorite. I swung my eyes back to see Coach Weber enter the room through the glass doors and quickly pull the curtains across. Without any preamble he had the woman in his arms.

"Stop!" I called out and Julian froze the image. "Is there any way to get a look at her?"

Julian rewound the images and we got a visual of the woman as she came through the door alone. He stopped the image and seemed to be concentrating. The indistinct became more solid until it was like she was actually in the room with us.

Julian panted as if he was running a marathon. "I can't hold this for long. Do you recognize her?"

I shook my head. "No, but there's something about her." I stepped closer and examined her face. "Is it just me or does she look too perfect?"

Julian stepped closer to get a look and groaned. "It's a glamor. That's not how she really looks."

I frowned as I looked closer at the beautiful woman in front of me.

"What's a glamor?"

"It's like a mask that some witches can create. It hides what they look like and they can take any appearance they like. Vanity being what it is, most of them choose a beautiful and young visage. You can usually tell because they make themselves look faultless. Everything is perfectly symmetrical, there are no blemishes, nothing is out of place."

"So, we don't know what she looks like," I couldn't help the disappointment I felt.

The images blinked out and Julian took a steadying breath. "No, we don't, but we do know that she is a very powerful witch. Only the strongest could do a glamor like that, and to hold it long enough to do whatever it was she was doing with Weber."

I was grateful that he refrained from going into details.

"What do we do now?"

Julian started hustling me out of the room. "Now, I need to get back to the werewolves. We have to speak to the coach again. If he was fooling around with a witch that strong, she would have definitely been capable of creating the magic required to enhance the team and fool the testers."

Once we were back in the car, I gave voice to something

that was bothering me. "Why would she have done it? I mean, it's a game of football. I can kind of understand her getting involved with Coach Weber. Sometimes women have really questionable taste in men. I've learned not to be surprised in that regard, but unless he was offering her something pretty extraordinary, I don't see a witch that powerful doing something like that for no benefit to themselves."

"That's a question we need to ask the coach," Julian replied. "I have a feeling that there's more going on here than we can see."

*a*fter Julian dropped me off at my home, I headed for the coven library. The last few days I had been neglecting my job and I knew that couldn't continue. Fortunately, I was given some latitude when it came to my duties, but I was going to need to ensure I didn't abuse it.

For the next several hours I worked in the back room of the library. As usual there were only a couple of people who turned up to use the facilities. Despite instituting a new set of rules which allowed greater access to the library, I found some were reluctant to enter what was considered a sacred place. We were getting to a more egalitarian system, but it was taking some time. Most of my day was spent alone, searching for books containing curses that the previous librarian had secreted away. So far, I had not been successful.

As the day grew later, I took a walk through the library, to ensure nothing had been moved out of place. As I moved past one of the outer areas, I felt a familiar wave of nausea hit me. I gripped my stomach and started searching the area. Every time this had happened before, I had found a curse lurking within the vicinity. It didn't take me long until I found the culprit. I pulled the grimoire down and started wiping away at the tendrils which were wrapped around it. I recognized this book. Back when I first arrived in Walker Bay, I had seen a dark aura around it. At the time Tilda had looked at it and declared that it was nothing more than a standard grimoire full of household spells. I didn't understand how it could have developed a curse. Once I'd ensured all the tendrils were gone, I put the book on a nearby table and started searching through every room of the library, worried about what I'd find.

Within an hour I had a pile of seventeen books on the table, all with signs that they had been cursed. I had no idea how this had happened. As I reached for my phone, I jumped as it rang in the silence. Before I could say anything, I heard Flora's voice holding an urgency I hadn't heard before.

"I need you to go home. I'll meet you there."

Without waiting for me to reply she hung up. I looked at the phone, looked at my pile of books and sighed. I had a feeling this was going to be one of those nights.

Flora was waiting for me outside my house when I arrived home, a box in her hands and a look of impatience on her face. This morphed to confusion when I started unloading books.

"What are you doing?"

"Let me get these in the house first and then I'll explain," I replied.

Once the task had been completed, I turned to my aunt. "A couple of hours ago I found that all these books had been cursed."

Flora's jaw dropped as she looked over the books. "How...?"

I threw up my hands, frustration coursing through me. "I have no idea how it happened. I know at least one of the books had caused me some concern before, but I have never seen any indication that it was actually cursed."

Flora shook her head as she studied the grimoires. I had destroyed the tendrils that had been clinging to them, but I knew that as long as these books existed, whatever curse was attached to them was still capable of causing mayhem.

"Could these be the grimoires that Isobel saved?"

I shook my head in answer to Flora's question. Isobel had been the previous librarian who had gone rogue. Rather than destroying grimoires with curses in them as dictated by the Conclave, she had saved them. I was still looking for that particularly evil collection of books.

"Until today I had never seen one of these books with any sign there was a curse attached. It's like they went evil overnight."

Flora frowned. "Are you sure? That doesn't make sense."

I threw myself down on the couch. "Of course, I'm sure. The second I walk past anything with a curse attached I feel it physically. There is no way this many books could have remained hidden from me, and unless somebody has managed to break through your wards, nobody has been in the library without me. I would have noticed if somebody was casting curses on my books."

It irritated me that once again my library had become the site of evil. I sighed as my eye drifted to the box Flora had brought with her.

"What's that?" I asked.

Flora smiled, a tired expression on her face. "That contains the championship rings of every non-werewolf player in the football team."

I stood up and opened the box, grimacing at the sight of tendrils crawling all over the bottom of it. "How did you get these?"

"Perks of being a coven leader," Flora replied. "People generally listen when you tell them something."

"Except werewolves," I murmured.

"Werewolves don't listen to anybody but themselves."

I could hear the frustration in Flora's voice.

"This would be easier if we could just tell people about the curses, wouldn't it?"

Flora shrugged. "Theoretically it would be, but people can be difficult even when they have all the facts. There's no guarantee they would hand over these items even if they knew they were cursed."

I went to put my hand in the box and hesitated. "We're destroying these, aren't we?"

Flora nodded. "Considering how amped up those boys are getting, I would suggest the sooner the better. There have been fights and arguments all over town. I heard Deputy Iversen threw a couple in the local jail cell so they'd cool off."

This was getting out of control. I started methodically destroying the rings. Once again, I marveled at the way I was able to crush them in my hand with such little effort. I had a feeling my powers were growing. Now, wasn't that a scary thought?

"You know, it would be better if you had cleared out a space in the basement. It's generally considered more appropriate to use your magic in a confined area. Helps you focus it."

"I'll get right on that," I commented, "just as soon as people stop throwing curses in this town and give me a decent chance to start renovating this place. Anyway, I've got to find the curse that you said was on this house before I start to do anything permanent."

Yes, my aunt had put me in a cursed house. I understood that she'd only put me in here because I was the one person who was immune to curses. Still, it was a little disturbing that she seemed so cavalier with my safety. Just as the last ring was destroyed there was a knock at my front door.

"You expecting anybody?" Flora asked, her tone guarded.

Considering the way my life was going, I wouldn't be surprised no matter who was at the front door. I breathed out a sigh of relief when I found Eamon. He held up a bag.

"Okay, I did what you wanted. I got the rings. Now would you mind telling me what the hell is going on with my people."

I looked around, anxious at the thought of Julian lurking close by. "Get in here and we'll explain."

A disgruntled Eamon followed me into the house and pulled up short when he saw Flora. His head swung back to me. "I am not going to like this explanation, am I?"

"Probably not," I sighed as I held out my hand for the bag. He passed them over and I put them on the table with the rest of the cursed items I was collecting.

"We believe a witch has been playing with magic to bump up the aggression levels in the football team. We think that they used the rings as a medium."

"You're telling me a witch is playing with the minds of werewolves?" Eamon growled.

"I'm saying there's a witch that's playing with everybody. She or he does not seem to discriminate."

Eamon scrubbed his hands down his face. "Aidan is going to lose his mind if he thinks witches are messing with werewolves."

"Like Sadie said, it isn't just werewolves," Flora inserted smoothly.

"What about my father makes you think that he's going to hear that part of the explanation?"

The man had a point.

"We're doing everything we can to find who did this," I replied.

"But you're no closer," Eamon said shrewdly.

My shoulders slumped. "No."

"What about the affair thing with Weber? He claims you're lying to stitch him up."

"Believe me, we're not." I said, my mind going back to what I'd witnessed in the hotel room. "I've seen what he was doing and who he was doing it with. I wish I hadn't."

Eamon raised an eyebrow. "The magister?"

I nodded. "He was able to show what happened in the room at the inn and I saw it all. I wish I had that kind of power. It was amazing."

Eamon sucked in a breath. "You're sounding a little too impressed by the magister for my liking."

I raised an eyebrow at the comment. "I'm working with him to try to ascertain what is going on in this town. I really don't like what you're insinuating."

"I'm not insinuating anything," Eamon said defensively. "I just wish you hadn't pulled the Conclave into this mess."

"And who should we have reported our suspicions to?" I retorted. "If we'd gone to the sheriff's office, Detective Hanlon would have been all over it. We may as well have gone straight to Aidan."

"You could have come to me."

Flora leaned forward. "Are you saying that you wouldn't have told the alpha?"

Eamon straightened. "I'm saying that I would have done the best thing for this town as well as my clan."

Flora sat back with a gleam in her eyes and I could see her mind working.

Eamon turned back to me. "What are you going to do now?"

I glanced back at the pile of items on my table. "Now we are going to spend the night cleansing these things, and hope that by tomorrow the football team will go back to being constructive members of society rather than the juvenile delinquents we have running around now."

"Sounds like a plan." Eamon started moving towards the door and then looked back, a concerned expression on his face. "Watch your back with the magister. I don't trust him."

I nodded. He wasn't the only one.

*O*nce Eamon left, I went back to the task of destroying the cursed items. The rings were easy. It was only when I came to the books that I hesitated.

"Is there a way to get rid of this curse without destroying the books?" I asked plaintively as I held the first of the grimoires in front of me.

The thought of willfully wiping out this kind of history and knowledge went against everything I believed in.

Flora placed a hand on my arm and looked up at me. "It has to be done."

I dropped my head. "I'm guessing fire would be the best way."

She nodded and with a heavy heart I set about starting a fire in the old fireplace. Despite my initial concerns, the fireplace seemed to be the one thing in the house that wasn't broken down, blocked, or just plain trying to kill me. Before long we had a lovely fire. I then proceeded to feed centuries of wisdom to the flames. As each book became ash, I got an image of people who had studied the grimoires and learned from their pages. There was no anger, no hostility, just a simple act of gaining knowledge.

I turned to Flora. "Something really strange is happening here. I don't understand..."

I was interrupted by her phone ringing. I could tell by the look on her face that it wasn't good news. She hung up the phone, grabbed my hand and dragged me to the front door.

"That was Dr Collias. He said that he's had an influx of patients with lesions on their bodies, similar to what Lisa had."

We raced to the clinic, only to be brought up short by the doctor standing out the front with a frown on his face.

"I may have acted too quickly by calling you. It seems to have been some temporary reaction. I think it may have been environmental. All the patients have suddenly healed, they're totally fine."

I felt sorry for the poor doctor who seemed completely flummoxed by the sudden turn of events. My eyes widened as the first of the patients walked out the door.

"I think we need to see these patients," I said as I stepped forward.

After a moment of confusion, Collias nodded his understanding. "You know something?"

I inclined my head in an attempt not to lie to the man who had been nothing but good to me since the day I was dragged into this town.

"I have an idea what might be happening, but I need to see all the patients that came in with lesions."

Dr Collias nodded and turned to enter the clinic. Flora and I followed behind him, and as we went from room to room my heart sank at the implications of what I saw. Despite Dr Collias' initial panicked phone call, all the patients were now fine with not a mark on them to indicate the reason why they had come rushing to the clinic. As I watched the confused medical staff at a loss to explain the sudden mass healing of the patients, I pulled Flora to one side and activated my troll doll.

"I saw these people in visions when I was destroying the grimoires. Every single person in here has used one of those books."

A confused expression settled on Flora's face. "That's not how curses work. You can't catch a curse like a cold."

If the leader of the coven didn't understand this, I had no chance of working it out.

"It explains the quick healing," she mused. "The second the curse was broken, the lesions would have started disappearing."

I looked up as I felt somebody watching me. The knowing expression on the doctor's face caused me to catch my breath "I think we have a problem."

"I need to speak to both of you now."

He kept his voice low, but there was no mistaking the command in the doctor's tone.

We followed him into his office, and he waited until the door was closed before asking the inevitable question. "What are you not telling me?"

Flora stepped forward. "We're not entirely sure what's happening. As soon as we have anything that you can use, we will tell you.

I could tell Dr Collias did not like her explanation by the anger that crept over his face. He slammed his hand down on the desk. "You are going to tell me what is happening. I can't take care of the people in this town if I'm hamstrung by secrets."

By the stunned look on Flora's face I assumed this was the first time that Dr Collias had questioned what she'd told him. I had to give her credit, she recovered quickly.

"You're right. Despite my best efforts, this seems to be

happening too often for us to hope to keep it quiet." She raised her head and looked the centaur square in the face. "There are curses being cast in Walker Bay. I am doing my best to keep up with them and negate their effects, but I am not sure why this is happening."

I appreciated my aunt's attempt to protect me, but I could tell just by looking at him that Dr Collias was too smart to take what she said at face value. His next words confirmed it.

"I have known you your entire life and because of that I know how important your niece is to you. It is for that reason alone that I am going to forgive that lie." He swung his head in my direction. "Now, I need you to explain what I can do for my patients."

I drew in a deep breath and gave Flora an apologetic look. "You need to make them as comfortable as possible and help them with pain. Ask them if they have been using any products that may have been purchased from a Traveler witch, and then you need to contact me immediately. There seems to be no discernible pattern to the people being struck down, and there is some concern that they only need to touch an affected object to feel the effects of the curse."

"Another curse," Collias rumbled. "Something very bad has entered this town." He narrowed his eyes as if trying to peer into my soul. "I need to know if that bad thing is you."

I hesitated, and in that moment Flora jumped in. "How dare you ask that? You have no idea what she has done to protect the people in this town or what it costs her."

Although I appreciated the defense, I had a feeling it was unnecessary. Despite his question, I didn't think Dr Collias really believed I caused the problems in Walker Bay. I did think he was a highly intelligent and well-read man who was using every single one of our reactions to narrow down exactly what I was. If he didn't know that I was a curse-breaker already, he soon would.

"One more thing," Collias said. "The magisters have been questioning my staff about what has been going on here. They don't have the jurisdiction to interview me, but they are suspicious. I would suggest you keep your distance from them."

His warning sent chills through me. "I wish I could."

One thing I was learning during my time in Walker Bay was that bad things always seemed to happen in the darkness of night. I'd also learned that trouble invariably ended up at my front door. I couldn't tell you what it was that woke me that night. It wasn't a pounding on my door like I would expect, it was a general unease like something was seriously wrong, and it was close.

I reached for the baseball bat that I kept behind my bedroom door. In the absence of any useable form of magic, I'd decided to go for a traditional method of protection. I crept down the stairs, hearing each creak from every loose tread on the way down and wishing I had found the time to do some decent renovations on this house. Upon reaching the front door I put my ear against it, hoping for some indication of what was disturbing me. All I heard was a groaning noise.

With a tight grip on the bat I eased the front door open and found a body slumped against it. As the door came wider, the body sprawled over the threshold and I got a good look at their face. I dropped to my knees beside him.

"Coach Weber," I breathed at the man who only twelve hours ago had wanted to hurt me badly. "What happened to you?"

Weber was covered in blisters that oozed blood. He opened his mouth as if to speak and more blood dribbled out of it.

"I'll get you help."

I went to move away so I could get my phone when he stretched out and grabbed my arm.

"Not safe," he managed to choke out. "They'll find me."

I dropped down to my knees. "Who will find you? Who did this to you?"

"I thought she loved me. I was going to leave my wife for her."

"What was her name?" I asked urgently.

Despite his pain a smile crossed his cracked lips. "Fausta."

"Where can I find her? Is she in town?" I fired off questions knowing my ability to get answers once anybody else arrived was limited.

"She isn't here. I can't breathe without her."

If I didn't have a sneaking suspicion that the coach was under some sort of love spell, I would have been impressed with his devotion to the woman who was probably trying to kill him. I pulled myself up and reached for my phone. "I'm calling for help," I said before punching in the number for the clinic.

Dr Collias answered, his voice surprisingly alert considering it was the early hours of the morning.

"I've got a werewolf on my doorstep covered in boils that are bleeding and I don't know why. I need medical help now."

I saw Weber reaching out his hand and I grasped it.

"I'm sorry," he cried as I settled next to him. "They were going to fire me."

"What did you do?" I asked gently, although I was pretty sure I already knew.

"Potion. In the boy's water. It was the only way for us to win."

I suppressed my natural disgust at the fact this man was doping children to keep his job.

"Where is she?"

Weber looked up at me with tear filled eyes, his expression full of desolation. "I can't find her. She left me alone and I can't live without her."

"Did she give you anything, a keepsake, something that you treasure?" I asked.

Weber frowned as the words I was saying got through to him. He pulled a blood-soaked chain from around his neck and gave it to me. Seeing the tendrils that normally caused me such discomfort almost made me smile. At least this I could fix. In one swift movement I put my hand behind my back and crushed the chain. A quick image of Weber and the woman from the hotel slammed into me, but this time I did get a feeling and it was indifference. Whoever this person was, she had not loved Doug Weber. She hadn't hated him either. She felt nothing for him, he was just an instrument for her to get what she wanted. Unfortunately, what she wanted still eluded me.

"What's going on here?"

I jumped as Julian loomed out of the darkness, and I didn't miss the fear in Weber as he gripped my hand tighter.

"He turned up on my doorstep, I've already called for help," I said as I surreptitiously wiped my dust-encrusted hand on the welcome mat.

As if to back up my claims we heard a siren. The ambulance pulled up at the front of my house and paramedics leapt out.

Weber's grip on my hand grew even tighter and the fear coming off him was palpable.

"You're going to be fine," I soothed. "Dr Collias is going to be able to help you."

I could already see that the boils were not looking quite so raw and angry, and I had a feeling that it wouldn't be too long before the curse's effect completely disappeared. I knew it would be better if that happened when he was in the safe hands of a medical professional. I figured there would be less questions that way, so over Weber's feeble protests, I helped get him into the back of the ambulance.

As we watched the ambulance leave, Julian looked over at me. "Are you okay?"

I gave a shaky laugh. "Course I'm okay, why would you think I'm not?"

"Because you look like you've walked out of a disaster zone."

I looked down at myself and found that my pajamas were covered in blood. Momentary panic hit me, and I turned away. "I need to clean up." I started to go back in the house but stopped when I realized Julian was following me. "What are you doing?"

Julian watched me as if concerned for my mental state. "I'm staying with you tonight. You need protection."

I put my hand up as my mind contemplated that ludicrous thought. "That is not going to happen. You are not now, nor will you ever be, welcome in my home." I knew I was being harsh, but I had always known that Julian did not get subtle. "And don't get any ideas about forcing your way into my house to provide this protection. The wards were done by Flora, and I know it may not look like it from the state of this house, but she's very protective of me. Those wards have a kick to them, just ask your sister."

I left Julian standing on the porch and closed the door

firmly behind me. It was the one thing in this house that I had absolute confidence would stand, and that was only because it had been replaced after being smashed in by an overwrought berserker werewolf.

"Go home, Julian," I called through the door. "I'm perfectly safe in here."

I gave a sigh of relief when I heard his footsteps walking away. A part of me knew that his offer had been sweet, but another part of me never wanted a magister to set foot in my home. I didn't even come close to trusting him enough to allow that to happen.

I grabbed a trash bag out of the kitchen and headed up to my bathroom. After a long hot shower, I finally began to feel clean. A quick call to Dr Collias confirmed that Coach Weber was in the process of healing and was sleeping comfortably. I could hear the unasked query in the doctor's voice, but I wasn't prepared to help him.

I went to crawl into bed when a sudden movement on the deck caught my eye. It didn't take me long before I worked out who my unwanted visitor was.

I pulled open the glass door. "What do you think you're doing?"

Julian struggled a little with his sleeping bag as he sat up. "I'm protecting you. What does it look like I'm doing? You won't let me in your house so this is the best I can do."

I raked my hand through my hair. "I don't want you here. I don't need you here. Why won't you listen to me?"

Julian pulled himself out of his sleeping bag and stood in front of me, his hands on my shoulders. "You just had a suspect in a case we are working on turn up on your front doorstep. That is not something that should happen. There are a hundred other places he should have gone to rather than here. The fact he did worries me. It means you're being targeted in some way. I won't sit by and let that happen."

If I wasn't so frustrated and tired, I would have thought his sentiment was sweet. I stepped back and he dropped his hands.

"Fine, if you insist on sleeping on my deck I won't stop you, but I'm still not inviting you in."

With that I stepped back in the house and closed the door, annoyed that I did not have a decent curtain I could pull across. I crawled into bed and turned my back on the glass doors, but I could still feel eyes watching me. I had a feeling I was making a mistake.

20

I groaned when I heard the pounding on my front door. After the night I'd just had I shouldn't have expected that I was going to have any chance of catching up on my sleep. I stumbled down the stairs and opened the door.

My eyes which had still been half-closed widened with surprise. "Detective Hanlon, what are you doing here?"

I should have realized that the smile on her face was not a good sign.

"Sadie Goodwin, you are under arrest," Hanlon announced as I was roughly turned around and my arms were yanked back and handcuffed. I winced as agony streaked up to my shoulders. When I was pulled back, I caught sight of the expression on the deputy who was restraining me. From the smile on his face I could tell he took a sadistic joy in causing me pain. I looked around at the deputies that Hanlon had decided to use. Every one of them was a werewolf. Considering how most werewolves felt about witches in general, and me in particular, I knew that choice had not been an accident. I started to feel fear.

"What the hell is going on here?"

I could see the authoritative voice startled Hanlon. For the first time in a very long while I was pleased to see Julian Bernauer. Although, with his clothes crumpled and his hair mussed he didn't exactly scream intimidation. After a second Hanlon's eyes gleamed.

"Well, well. This is surprising."

"Not really," Julian said smoothly. "I do live right next door. When an inept police force decides to raid somebody in the street, they're generally not subtle. You woke me up."

I noted that he neglected to inform them he was coming down from my deck and not from across my yard.

"Miss Goodwin is being charged with the murder of Doug Weber."

My head snapped up. "What? That's not possible. He was going to be fine." I'd broken the curse. I was sure that the boils had been healing. I would never have let him go to Dr Collias if I thought for a moment there was a chance the curse still had him.

"Doug Weber died an hour ago from whatever spell you put him under."

If the situation had not been so dire, I would have laughed. "I can't do spells. Everybody knows that."

I could tell from the look on Hanlon's face that no matter what I said, it wasn't going to make a bit of difference. She had been wanting to get rid of me since the moment she first found out about the Destined Beloved prophecy. Her obsession with Conall Tolan was going to destroy her. I just hoped she didn't take me down as well.

"According to reports, when the paramedics got here you were covered in blood."

I grimaced at the reminder. "He was covered in boils and some of them were bleeding. I was trying to help him."

Hanlon waved a hand in the air. "You can explain it all

when we get you to the sheriff's office." She pulled out a piece of paper. "This is a warrant to search your house."

Despite my intense anger at what was happening, my innate sense of fairness wouldn't let that statement go without a warning. "I would suggest you contact Flora first. She set the wards for this house. They're pretty twitchy. I'm not sure if she put an exemption in for all emergency responders."

For the first time I saw Hanlon's look of triumph falter.

"I'd listen to her," Julian said as he leaned against the wall, his arms crossed as if he didn't have a care in the world. I wondered if anybody else could see the tension coursing through him. "Flora Harstone is as strong a witch as you're ever likely to come across. I hate to think what punishments she has put in place for anybody who dares to threaten her niece."

I know he was trying to help, but I could have told him to save his breath. Detective Hanlon's path was set, and nothing was going to make her change course. I was unceremoniously yanked off the porch. As I lost my footing, I was shocked when a deputy stepped up and prevented me from hitting the ground. I looked up into the vaguely familiar face of Deputy Diaz.

"I'll take her," he snarled, and the other deputies backed off. As usual, with werewolves the dominance hierarchy ruled everything.

"Make sure she is comfortable," Hanlon called out as Diaz dragged me towards the patrol car.

"I'm guessing she doesn't really mean that," I muttered.

Diaz grunted. I was surprised when he protected my head as he shoved me into the back seat. "I don't want to hear one word out of you," he snarled as he slammed the door shut.

I watched as Julian argued with Hanlon on my porch, and I saw him pull out his phone. I just hoped that he was doing something useful because I had a bad feeling that the were-wolf clan had finally found a chance to get rid of me.

When we were halfway to the sheriff's office, Diaz pulled the car over into an empty parking lot. Fear gripped me as I wondered what was going to happen. He got out of the driver's seat and pulled me out. I steeled myself, waiting for a blow that I knew was coming. I froze as he undid the handcuffs.

"What are you doing?" I croaked as I rubbed my wrists which had been abraded badly by the way the restraints had been put on.

Diaz's glared at my wrists. "There was no need for them to do that."

I frowned in confusion. "What are you talking about?"

The deputy's eyes rose to mine. "They didn't need to hurt you like that. It wasn't right."

I knew it wasn't right, but some people abuse the power they are given. It was simply a fact of life. As soon as I saw that Hanlon had only brought werewolf deputies, I knew something bad was going to happen. I had a feeling this arrest had nothing to do with Doug Weber's death, and everything to do with Aidan Tolan's animosity towards his son and me.

Diaz sighed. "I need to take you in, but I promise I won't hurt you. I just wanted to get those things off your wrists."

I took a closer look at the concerned expression on Diaz's face and I saw a cop who wanted to do the right thing. He was just trapped by a system where justice sometimes took a back seat to political ambition.

"It's okay," I nodded. "I understand, and thank you for taking those off."

I got in the back seat and stared ahead.

After a minute of watching me, Diaz got back in the car and continued driving, neither of us saying another word.

I was surprised when we drove around the rear of the sheriff's office. It all became clear to me when Diaz pulled me through the back door to the part of the building which housed the jail cells. I had a feeling he was hoping to keep a lid on this situation until he had an opportunity to explain what was happening to some of the deputies who were not quite so under the thrall of Detective Hanlon like the werewolves were.

I think I hadn't quite grasped what was happening until the moment Diaz gently pushed me into a cell and I realized something. The floor of the jail cell was cold. Tears pricked my eyes as I registered that my feet were bare. I had been dragged out of my home in my pajamas and no shoes. That couldn't be right.

I looked up at Diaz and he must have seen my distress.

"I'll get you some clothes," he promised, "and some food. Is there anything you'd prefer?"

I was about to answer when we both heard footsteps coming down the hallway. Diaz dropped his head and I could see that this was not the way he had hoped things would play out.

"Hey, Diaz," a voice called out and hope surged through me. Pike was here.

"You guys seem keen today. I've never come in and seen so many of your shift out on the road, and you've already arrested somebody. Who is it?"

Diaz stepped back and Pike got a look at me huddled in the cell wearing only my pajamas.

"You son of a…What do you think you're doing?" He raised his voice to a yell. "Iversen, get in here!"

Karl walked in, an annoyed expression on his face. "What is your problem this time, Pike? I swear, you are the most high maintenance…What in the hell?"

Pike pointed at Diaz. "This idiot has arrested her."

Despite my misery, I didn't feel that was fair. "Technically, Detective Hanlon arrested me. If you want to make somebody's life a misery, I would suggest you start with her."

Iversen's attention snapped back to Deputy Diaz. "Explain. Now."

Diaz started reciting what I was guessing was going in a report somewhere.

"At two o'clock this morning, Sadie Goodwin contacted the clinic to inform them that Doug Weber was on her front porch and needed medical assistance. When the paramedics arrived they found both Doug Weber and Sadie Goodwin covered in blood."

"His blood," I interrupted. "He was covered in boils and they were oozing blood."

"That's disgusting," Pike said before swinging his gaze back to Diaz. "Please continue."

"Doug Weber was transported to the clinic where he was treated," Diaz kept talking as if we hadn't said anything.

Karl shook his head. "I'm not seeing why that means Hanlon arrested Sadie," Karl growled as he unlocked the cell and took off his jacket, wrapping it around my shoulders.

"Doug Weber died an hour ago. Sadie was determined to be the most likely suspect. Detective Hanlon called in some deputies and arrested her."

Karl was silent as his attention was taken by the marks on my wrist. "Who handcuffed her?" His voice was low and menacing.

Diaz looked pained. "It was Rogers."

"Why am I not surprised," hissed Pike. "He's a blight on this department. The sheriff gave him one more chance. If he survives doing this, it will be a miracle."

Diaz inclined his head. "The fact remains, she is under arrest for murder. Nothing you do can change that unless evidence is found which exonerates her."

Karl's head snapped up. "I am the one in charge of this department. While the sheriff's away it is my decision who is arrested and who is not."

"Not this time, Deputy." I should have known Detective Hanlon would be arriving soon. "Now, isn't this a cozy scene? Unfortunately, nobody can protect your precious witch this time."

I could feel Karl vibrating with anger next to me. "What are you talking about? This is still my town until the sheriff comes back."

Hanlon sneered. "I arrested Sadie Goodwin under the powers of the State Police. I borrowed some deputies, but make no mistake, this is my arrest and there is nothing you can do about it." She peered over at Diaz. "This cell is to be locked at all times and you are not to let her out of your sight."

With that parting shot, Detective Brigitte Hanlon strutted out with all the confidence of a woman who believed she had won.

"Out," Diaz said as he gestured at Karl.

"So, you're falling in line with the clan, are you?" sneered Pike. "I thought you were a better cop than that."

For the first time I saw anger on Diaz's face. "I am a better cop than that. That's how I know that whining about this situation is not going to help her. If you want to really get her out of here, you need to find the evidence that absolves her of this crime." He ran a hand through his hair. "I will stay here and I swear no harm will come to her on my watch."

I could see the indecision on both Karl's and Pike's faces.

"He's right," I said, knowing they wouldn't leave me unless I told them to go. "I'll be fine here." I tried to give a brave smile but from the looks they gave me, I was pretty sure I'd missed the mark. "Go, please."

The two men reluctantly moved away.

"Anything happens to her, I'm coming after you," Pike growled as he passed Diaz.

"You won't have to," the werewolf replied as if giving a solemn vow. "The only way anyone will get to her is if I am dead."

21

"Why are you helping me?" I asked Diaz. "I always figured that all of the werewolves hated me on principle. Why don't you?"

Diaz leaned back and closed his eyes. "My older brother was one of those that were afflicted by the plague." He straightened up and looked me in the eye. "You were at the clinic with the coven leader every day, bringing relief to those affected. Nobody died after you and Flora started working with the doctor. I don't know what you did, but I believe you saved his life. For that, I am eternally in your debt. If I can repay a small part of that debt now, I will."

"I'm guessing that doesn't extend to helping me escape," I said, only half joking.

"Escaping will not help you. Only a full exoneration will get you out of this mess," Diaz said, his tone deadly serious.

There went that hope.

"Why isn't Hanlon interrogating me yet?"

Diaz smiled humorlessly. "Despite all appearances to the contrary, Hanlon isn't an idiot. She knows once this becomes official, Flora will bring all the resources of the coven to your side. The second they start interviewing you, your advocate gets involved. That is the last thing she wants with a case this flimsy. She's going to keep you here as long as she can and gather every piece of evidence she can find until she has something that resembles an iron-clad prosecution. Only then will she talk to you."

I was not looking forward to that happening.

Diaz cocked his head as if hearing something and sighed loudly. "Great, this is the last thing I need."

I strained and it took a few minutes before I heard noise heading in our direction. I grimaced when I recognized Tilda's raised voice. It didn't take long for two of the people I cared for the most to be looking through the bars at me. You could almost feel the fury simmering in the room. Something needed to be said before there was bloodshed.

"It isn't his fault." I pointed at Diaz. I couldn't do much from in here, but I could make sure the one werewolf that had shown me kindness was not the one they focused their rage on.

Flora didn't take her eyes off me as she directed her question to Diaz.

"What is the reason for this?" Her voice was low and calm, but everybody could hear the threat in it.

Diaz repeated his report to Flora, and I was pretty sure it was word for word. Meanwhile, Tilda grasped my hand through the bars, her expression anguished.

"It's going to be okay," I murmured, trying to soothe my closet friend.

"She isn't going to stop until she destroys you," Tilda whispered, a bleak desperation in her tone.

"We're not going to let that happen." Flora's voice cut through our whispered conversation. She focused on Diaz. "Leave. We've brought clothes. She needs to get changed."

"No, Ma'am," Diaz replied. "I will not be leaving the prisoner."

I had to admire the guy. Most people I knew were not willing to stand up to Flora. The next step was usually her dominance power, and I had previously seen how much Diaz hated being subjected to it when Aidan Tolan had tried to make a point.

"Don't," I said to Flora as I could see the anger snapping in her eyes. "He doesn't deserve it. He's just trying to do the right thing."

Flora took in a shaky breath as if trying to control the rage, and Diaz sent me a look of gratitude.

"I'll turn around," he said apologetically.

It wasn't much, but I figured it was the best I was going to get. While I was changing into some decent clothes, I couldn't help but feel the anguish coming from Flora and Tilda.

"I'm fine," I said as I zipped up my boots, grateful that my feet were now protected from the cold. I wasn't sure why that was the indignity I was focusing on when there were so many others. "Karl and Pike are looking for a way to get me out of here."

Flora nodded. "I've contacted Tarquin. He's started working on a way to not just get you out of this, but to make sure Detective Hanlon can never pull a stunt like this again."

That sounded ominous, and you know what? I was good with that. Brigitte Hanlon had finally reached the point where I was no longer able to excuse her animosity towards me because of her hurt at losing Conall. Anything Flora wanted to unleash on that woman was fine with me.

"What is going on here? I leave town for a week and everything goes to hell."

Tilda rolled her eyes as her grandmother walked into the area. I know she was annoyed that Maude felt that she couldn't handle the Lisa situation, but she was never going to win that argument. That reminded me.

"How is Lisa doing?" I asked Tilda.

"Lisa's doing a lot better than you are," Maude replied before her granddaughter could. "Seriously, how do you end up with a werewolf dying on your front porch?"

"He didn't die on my front porch," I retorted. "He was perfectly fine when he was put into that ambulance. He was supposed to recover fully at the clinic."

Flora's head snapped up and I could see the unspoken question in her eyes. I inclined my head to confirm that another curse had been involved and she blew out a breath.

I looked up to find Diaz watching us, a speculative gleam in his dark eyes. I deliberately looked away. The last thing I needed was another person curious about what I could and couldn't do.

Flora noticed my worried expression and she turned to Diaz. "Deputy Greensmith will be taking over your duties in protecting Sadie."

I couldn't help but notice the fact she said protecting and not guarding.

Diaz drew himself up to his full height. "I have been charged with watching the prisoner. You do not have a say in that."

The smile Flora gave the werewolf was deadly. "You would be wise, Deputy Diaz, not to be so quick to ally yourself to Detective Hanlon. She seems to have a self-destructive streak."

Diaz eyed Flora steadily. "I am not allied to Detective Hanlon. I take my job very seriously and have sworn to make sure the prisoner is protected. That still stands."

I could see Flora struggling with this turn of events, but then she made a decision.

"Very well, the two of you will protect her."

She glanced behind Diaz and I saw Deputy Jim Green-smith in the doorway. I could understand why Flora wanted him to guard me. Although he was a sworn deputy, he was also a member of her coven. Flora would have difficulty trusting anyone else with my safety. This situation was proving to be just as much about the political system in Walker Bay as it was about the justice system. My aunt grasped my hand and looked me deep in the eyes.

"We are going to get you out of this." She lowered her voice. "And I am going to make sure that nothing like this ever happens to you again."

Even though I knew the witches couldn't hear her, I was aware that Diaz could, and by the way his eyes widened I could tell he heard the threat that was implicit in that statement.

I put on a smile that I knew wasn't fooling anybody. "I'm going to be fine. Karl and Pike are on this. If anybody can get me out of this mess, it will be them."

I trusted my friends to do everything they could to help, but there was a part of me that was very scared. It took a bit more reassurance before the women were willing to leave, but when they did, I sighed in relief. That left me with the two deputies for entertainment, and I was desperately in need of entertainment.

"How are things going with Marigold?" I had noticed that after recovering from the plague, Deputy Greensmith and the coven healer had been spending a lot of time together.

"Fine," Jim clipped out.

"Just fine?" I whined. "I need more than that. If you haven't noticed, I'm stuck in a jail cell and Diaz isn't the talk-ative type. You need to give me something."

Jim looked over at me and I waited expectantly. "No, I don't. I was asked to protect you. Sharing my private life does not come under my list of duties."

Well, that was rude, considering I had severe doubts that Jim would have ever got over his own insecurities and asked the healer out if I hadn't intervened. I was taking their matchmaking as a highlight of my quest to find my powers.

"Do you really think discussing his romantic life is a worthwhile use of your time?"

I looked up to see Julian and his team of magisters in the doorway, and here was me trapped in a cell with no way out.

"Not much else to do," I replied, hoping that I wasn't betraying in any way how much their presence concerned me.

Both Julian and Liam had the professional magister expression down perfectly. Nobody would be able to guess what they were thinking or feeling. Magister Penelope Hartford was another matter altogether. I didn't think there was a force powerful enough to contain the gleeful expression I could see on her face at the sight of my predicament.

"I need to speak to the prisoner in private."

I really wish Julian had said that in a different way.

"That's not going to happen," drawled Diaz as he crossed his arms.

I could see Julian was frustrated at the fact that he was not the one calling the shots for a change. He stepped closer to the bars.

"I need to know what Doug Weber said to you."

I tried very hard not to flinch at his query. The problem was that I was currently in a jail cell for a crime I had not committed. I was surrounded by five people, none of whom I came close to completely trusting. I would never be able to trust the magisters, simply because I was hiding the fact I was one of those rogue witches they were supposed to hunt down. Despite Diaz's seeming willingness to protect me, I had a feeling that his loyalty was more to the rule of law than anything else. An admirable quality, but not exactly something I was able to place my faith in considering how it was currently being used against me. Deputy Greensmith had been put in here because Flora trusted him. I didn't know him well enough to do the same. This meant there was not one person in this area who I was willing to confide in.

"He didn't say anything."

"You expect us to believe you?" Magister Hartford sneered.

"The man had blood pouring out of his mouth," I replied. "He wasn't really in a position to engage in idle conversation. I was more worried about getting him some medical assistance than in finding out why he ended up on my porch."

The enmity I saw in Penelope Hartford's face almost made me flinch. It confirmed what I already knew. This was not a woman that I could ever trust.

I stepped away from the bars and sat on the cot, crossing my legs as I watched the three magisters.

"Just so you know, Peter Martel is also missing."

My head snapped up in surprise at Julian's announcement. "The assistant coach? I don't understand."

Julian sighed. "Neither do we." He glanced at Diaz. "The werewolves are closing ranks. We aren't permitted to speak to any of them and Eamon Tolan is ignoring any attempt to contact him."

I stared up at the ceiling, frustration building. I could not understand what was happening in this town. It was like everything was falling apart and we couldn't seem to stop it, no matter what we did.

"Is this a private party, or can anybody join?"

I had to admit that of all the people I expected to visit me in a jail cell, Arthur McClune was somewhere close to the bottom.

I waved him over. "Sure, join the party. I'm kind of hoping you brought food, because nobody else has."

McClune dug around in his jacket pocket and passed me a protein bar. "I always carry one around for emergency situations."

"You are a prince among men." I bit into the bar with relish before questioning how long it had been in that pocket.

From the looks of Diaz and Greensmith, neither were willing to leave their posts long enough to feed me, and I'd be a bit leery about accepting food from the magisters.

Julian was the first to react to the appearance of the hermit. "Are you going to introduce us to your friend?"

I waited until I finished my mouthful. "This is Arthur McClune. He's teaching me the history I would have learned if I went to school in Walker Bay."

I gestured towards the magisters. "These lovely people are Julian Bernauer, Liam Rigby and Penelope Hartford. They are the magisters that were sent by the Conclave to keep an eye on the town and make sure we're all okay."

McClune raised an eyebrow. "Really?" He turned to the magisters. "Considering the coven leader's niece is currently incarcerated on a spurious charge, I would think you would be better served doing your job, rather than harassing her."

Julian looked surprised by McClune's confrontational attitude. I wasn't. I was pretty sure the man was fine with making enemies with everybody. That reminded me, I should probably make sure he left before Karl came back. The last thing I needed was to add to what was already a stressful day.

"I'll be back later," Julian promised.

I really wished he wouldn't. "I'm fine," I said firmly. "I have plenty of people who are trying to get to the bottom of this. If you find anything you think will be useful, could you please pass it along to Flora or Deputy Iversen. Both of them are working to find out what happened."

Julian nodded sharply and walked out of the room with the other magisters close behind him. At the doorway Liam hesitated as if he wanted to say something but then thought better of it and followed the others.

"You really do have an eclectic collection of people in your life," mused Arthur before settling himself into a chair opposite the cell. "Now where did we end up?"

22

The only benefit to having McClune drone on about the history of witchcraft for five straight hours had been watching Diaz's and Greensmith's faces as they constantly checked the clock on the wall. Since he had a captive audience, the hermit didn't seem to feel there was any point in trying to make the lesson interesting to keep my attention. It shouldn't have been a great surprise that I fell asleep the moment he left, despite my uncomfortable surroundings. If he'd accomplished anything it was to bore me into insensibility.

I was woken when hands gripped my shoulders and I was dragged from the cot. I hit the cement floor hard, just managing to hold my head up to prevent it smashing into the ground.

"What…?"

I forced my head up and looked into the sadistic face of the werewolf who had handcuffed me so brutally earlier in the morning.

"Don't touch her, Rogers."

I glanced over to see Diaz being held down by three men,

only one of whom was wearing a deputy's uniform. He was struggling against his captors, but despite his best efforts he wasn't getting anywhere. Greensmith's body was lying unmoving on the ground.

A hand crashed into my cheek and my head snapped back.

"Shut up, Diaz. This has been a long time coming. It's because of her that Brian's in jail."

I wiped my hand across my mouth and grimaced at the blood. I kept silent as I had a feeling that pointing out that Brian Tolan was in jail because he murdered two people and attempted to murder me was not the most prudent course of action.

Rogers squatted down and stared at me. "Brian was going to be alpha and you ruined it."

I didn't say a word, but my mind was racing. Eamon was the eldest son and the one expected to become the next alpha. I knew that some in the community were looking forward to that day when they would have a more even-handed alpha of the werewolf clan. Nobody in their right mind would think that the psychotic Brian was a better option for the position.

Rogers pulled me up and slammed me against the wall, his hand pressing against my throat. "Now, you are going to tell me why Doug Weber ended up on your porch, what he said to you, and why he died."

I struggled against the hold, gasping for breath. "I don't know."

He pushed his face close to mine until I could feel his breath on my cheek. "You may think you're protected, little witch, but you're not. There are people in this town who would be quite happy if you simply no longer existed." To make his point he squeezed a bit tighter and I could see the room starting to gray around the edges.

Rogers let go of my throat suddenly and I dropped to the ground, gasping for breath. I looked up to find that Diaz had managed to loosen the grip of his captors and was putting up quite a fight against insurmountable odds. Rogers slammed shut the door to my jail cell and went to help his friends. He hit Diaz from behind, stunning the man long enough for the others to pin him down. He kicked the deputy in the side.

"You've made a bad choice, Diaz. No matter what you do, she's going to die."

I felt a jolt of power come from somewhere inside me and I frowned as I tried to work out what it was.

"What are you smiling about?" Rogers barked.

I hadn't realized that I was smiling but I could understand why. "You're the one who made a bad choice," I croaked.

Rogers stepped towards the jail cell door and I braced myself for the beating that was coming. I knew I only had to hold out a little while longer as help was on its way. Rogers' head snapped up as a howl drifted from the parking lot behind the sheriff's office. He nodded to one of the men standing over Diaz. "Check what that is."

As the thug reached the back door it came flying off its hinges and a creature from the darkest of nightmares came through. A bizarre hybrid between human and animal, there was no way to work out exactly what is was. All you could say was that it was huge and it was terrifying. Except to me. To me it looked like the most beautiful thing I'd ever seen in my entire life.

"What...?" Deputy Rogers' face was filled with fear, and he had good reason to be afraid. In the enclosed area, the sight of the monster that was usually his boss was even more intimidating than usual.

I knew that the werewolves were aware that Sheriff Tolan was a berserker. I was also aware that the fact very few had seen him in his berserker state meant that they might not fully understand the implications of that situation. It looked like Deputy Rogers was seriously rethinking some assumptions that he had made. He backed up as the sheriff threw the three men who had attacked Diaz into the wall, barely noticing what he was doing. His eyes were focused on Rogers and I felt a certain satisfaction at the whimper of fear that came from the sadistic cop. In a second, the sheriff was on him and I winced at the first crunch of a bone breaking. The scream of pain shook me out of my daze, and I crawled over to the side of the cell nearest to where Diaz was pulling himself up.

I reached my hand through the bars and grabbed Diaz's arm. "You need to let me out now."

"Are you crazy?" For the first time I saw Diaz's calm demeanor crack. "At the moment you're the safest person in here. I'd be tempted to join you if I didn't know that he would rip me apart the second I moved in your direction."

"I'm also the only person who can stop this," I said urgently. "If you don't let me out, people will start dying very soon."

It wasn't that I particularly cared about Rogers being killed, but I was concerned about the repercussions for Sheriff Tolan if he killed one of his deputies. Deciding that I must know what I was doing, but not willing to put himself in a situation where the sheriff saw him as a threat to me, Diaz slid me the keys to the jail cell. I pulled myself up and headed for the door. With my hands shaking, it took me a bit longer to unlock the door than I would have liked. By the time I had it opened, Rogers was a broken and bleeding shell of a man on the floor.

"Conall," I called softly, knowing that he would hear me.

The monster, reluctant to walk away from his prey, turned slowly in my direction. I stepped up to him and placed a hand over where I was assuming his heart was.

"You need to step back," I murmured. "I'm safe now. Nothing will be served by you killing him and we need to know why he did this."

Despite all evidence to the contrary, I did not believe that Rogers attacked two deputies and a prisoner to satisfy his own brutal urges. I think there was definitely something else going on here and we needed answers. Clawed hands curled around my shoulders as the pale blue eyes that I recognized as my Destined Beloved peered into my own. I closed my eyes knowing what would happen next. A bright light flashed, and I heard groaning as the sheriff made the change from monster to man. I grunted as his weight slumped against me, not sure if I could hold him. As seemed to be the norm when the change hit him, I could see his head leaning towards me, his eyes focused on my lips. For the first time I pulled myself out of his embrace before he could kiss me and stepped away towards the unconscious Greensmith. I checked his pulse and called out for Diaz.

"He's alive, we need to get help in here now."

Diaz pulled himself up, his left arm hanging awkwardly by his side. "On it."

I pulled off my jacket and rolled it in a ball, putting it under the deputy's head. I could feel Conall's eyes on me, but I refused to look up. Tears were gathering in my eyes, but I had no idea whether they were because of the shock, the pain or whether I was just over the whole paranormal experience. Before I'd been kidnapped and dragged to this place, I had lived a boring life, filled with grief and monotony. I had never thought I would miss those days, but right now I just wanted to catch a small piece of the calm and certainty that I had back then. I looked at the carnage around me and drew in a shaky breath. I had a feeling it would not be happening soon.

23

*I*t didn't take long to discover that Rogers and his friends had managed to intimidate the office staff who were the only people who had been left in the building. That had been the reason that nobody had come to our aid during the entire debacle. Once Diaz had put out a call for help, deputies started flooding back, although several of the werewolves were nowhere to be seen. Karl and Pike were apoplectic when they arrived on the scene.

"I'm going to kill him," rumbled Karl.

I was hoping he meant Rogers, because Diaz had lived up to his end of the bargain and done everything he could to protect me.

Due to the fact that Walker Bay only had one ambulance, and Diaz and I really weren't keen on sharing it with the bloody mess that used to be Deputy Rogers, we opted to be driven in the sheriff's truck to the clinic. I still had barely spoken to the sheriff and I could see him watching me in the rear-view mirror. I knew we needed to talk but I was feeling too raw right now. I closed my eyes and leaned my head against the window, uncaring that I was probably going to leave a bloody streak there.

When we reached the clinic, I was quickly put in a room and a nurse started tending to my many scrapes and bruises. She cleaned me up quickly and efficiently, barely saying a word for which I was profoundly grateful. I was surprised when Dr Collias walked in and dismissed her.

He turned to me and frowned. "I can't believe this happened."

I gave him a watery smile. "You and me both. What's the world coming to when you can't even be safe in a jail cell?"

Collias didn't smile at my pathetic attempt at a joke so I changed the focus of the conversation.

"How are Greensmith and Diaz?"

Collias started checking me to see if anything was more hurt than I was letting on. I should have told him not to worry. I was not being brave today.

"Deputy Greensmith was stunned and then kicked while he was on the ground. He's suffered a severe concussion, but he is now in the care of the coven healer. I think his biggest complaint will be that he is going to be smothered over the next week." He drew in a sharp breath as I winced at his fingers probing a particularly painful spot. "Deputy Diaz literally had his arm pulled out of its socket."

"I'm not surprised," I murmured. "He was fighting really hard to protect me."

Collias grunted. "Then at least the werewolves can take some honor out of this day."

That didn't sound good. I knew the last thing I should care about at this moment was the political situation in Walker Bay, but it seemed to color everything.

"How about Rogers?"

Anger such as I had never seen crossed the doctor's face.

"Rogers will live to face the consequences of his actions, but he will carry the scars."

I figured he was lucky to get out of this situation with his life. I just hadn't wanted to make things worse with another dead body.

When Collias finished his examination, he looked deeply in my eyes. "You're just holding on, aren't you?"

"I'm fine," I replied robotically.

Collias shook his head. "No, you're not. You've been through a traumatic event and you have to know that holding it in isn't going to do you any favors."

I gave him what I hoped was a reassuring smile and patted him on the arm. "Don't worry, I know what I'm like. The second I find somebody bigger and stronger than me, I'll probably fall apart. I just have to hold it together until that moment."

Collias sighed, looking very unimpressed with my plan. "I would suggest you find that person soon."

I intended to.

He left me in the room with strict instructions to have somebody else take me home and keep an eye on me. I put my clothes back on and straightened my shoulders. I figured I just needed to hang on for another twenty minutes and then I'd be home and able to fall apart the way I really wanted to.

I hesitated at the door of my room as I heard raised voices on the other side.

"You stay away from her," Conall growled. "She is mine to protect."

"And you've been doing a spectacular job of it so far," drawled Julian who seemed to have showed up.

I pushed through the door, irritated that once again I was the subject of male posturing.

"I need you both to back off," I bit out. I turned to the sheriff. "Thank you for saving me." I couldn't help the formality in my voice or the stiff way I was holding myself. I just needed to get myself through the next few hours and then I would start making decisions.

I looked up as the door to the clinic opened and Flora hurried towards me, flinging her arms around me. Despite my attempts to deal with this situation, the second I felt those arms I burst into tears. It looked like Flora was my bigger and stronger person. It hit me that I might not be going to the safety of my home. Despite what happened, I was still under arrest. I might be sent back to the jail cell. At that thought I knew I had to pull it together. I wiped a hand over my eyes and stepped back from Flora's embrace, although I grasped her hand, still needing that comfort.

"What happens now?"

I was surprised to see a bleakness in Conall's eyes, and I braced myself for more bad news. I was surprised when it was Flora that answered.

"You will be going home," she said strongly, as if daring anybody to contradict her. I wasn't going to say a word. If Detective Hanlon wanted me back in that cell, I didn't intend to go peacefully.

With a gentle hand Flora started leading me out of the clinic. Conall stepped forward but was stopped by Flora shaking her head. I didn't even have it in me to say goodbye to the two men. I let Flora bundle me in her car and she drove me home.

The first thing I did was peel off my clothes and have a shower. While the water flowed over me, my mind played back what had happened in the jail cell. I'd been in life-threatening situations before, but I'd never felt as trapped as I did there, like there was no possibility of me ever getting out. I was having trouble breathing and all of a sudden my bathroom seemed too small. I flicked off the water and quickly dried off. Throwing on some clothes, I walked through my bedroom, opened the glass doors and took in the view over the bay, breathing deeply in an effort to still the panic racing through me.

"Tarquin is in the process of filing a lawsuit for what happened today."

I didn't turn when I heard Flora's voice, but I could feel my heartbeat slowing down. Knowing she was still there soothed me in a way nothing else could.

"I'm not interested in bankrupting the sheriff's department," I said.

"The lawsuit is not against the sheriff's department. Detective Hanlon arrested you under her powers as a State police officer to avoid the sheriff's jurisdiction. Tarquin's going after her individually and the state as a whole. She deserves it. The evidence against you was too flimsy and she ignored that because of her personal feelings towards you and the sheriff."

I stepped back into the room and closed the doors. Walking towards my bedside table, I grabbed my troll doll and activated it. "He'd been cursed. I don't know why he ended up on my porch, but he told me that he'd been dosing the boys with a potion from some witch that he'd fallen in love with named Fausta. She was the one who put the curse on him."

"Fausta?" Flora queried.

"Do you know her?" I asked, confused by the look on her face.

"I doubt it," she replied. "Fausta is a name from ancient legends. It is usually associated with deceivers. I can't think of many witches who would willingly name their child that."

"Fake name," I mused. "Makes sense since she was using a fake face."

Flora raised an eyebrow as if questioning that statement.

"When Julian and I tracked down the hotel that Coach Weber had been using to meet his mistress, and Julian did the spell where you can see what happened in a place, we saw him with the woman. It looked like she was using some glamor spell to hide who she was. When I broke the curse, I got an image of her with him."

"You broke the curse?"

I nodded as I remembered back. "She'd given him a chain to wear around his neck. I destroyed it in my hand like I've been doing with the rings. I could see the boils getting better. I thought if they disappeared while he was in medical care there would be less questions. I thought the curse was gone."

Flora came up behind me and rubbed a soothing hand on my back. "Maybe the curse just didn't break properly. It must have been stressful and…"

"That's not how this works," I growled as I pulled away from her and paced across the room. "People are not supposed to die from curses on my watch. I find whatever medium the curse uses, and I destroy it. Everybody's supposed to go home happy and healthy. Hopefully they'll also learn to be a better person."

Flora's expression was full of sympathy. "You cannot win every time. It's impossible. If you start thinking that is going to happen, you will go mad."

"It was broken," I insisted. "I crushed the chain in my hands. There is no way he should have died." I sat on the edge of my bed. "I messed up somehow, didn't I? It's because I can't do any other magic. It's affecting my curse breaking abilities."

Flora sat down and put her arm around me. "You did all you could do. What happened was caused by somebody else. You need to stop blaming yourself."

In my head I knew she was right, but the guilt just kept eating at me.

Flora stood up and pulled back the covers. "You need sleep. Things will look better in the morning."

I crawled into bed and closed my eyes. I really hoped she was right.

24

*T*he next morning found me sitting on one of the few stable areas of my deck, watching the sun rise over the bay. When my aunt had said I could live in this house, it was with the knowledge that it came with a curse built in. Flora had informed me that if I could find the curse and get rid of it, she would give me the house. Since I'd started living in Walker Bay I had been so busy, and as the curse didn't affect me, I had ignored it. Halfway through my restless night I had decided that was going to change.

After my favorite spot to watch the sunrise had been tainted with a murder, I had found that I was just as happy opening the doors to my bedroom and stepping out onto this deck. As long as I kept well away from the rotted floor-boards, I was safe. I hoped. In my mind I could picture how this deck would one day look. I could see myself having dinner up here with my friends while the sun was setting. I ruthlessly squelched the rebellious thoughts of being up here with Conall that floated across my consciousness. I had plans for this house, but first I had to get rid of a curse.

I knew I was using my ideas for the house as a way to shy

away from thinking about anything that had happened in the last couple of days. I scrubbed my hands over my face. That was the coward in me talking. I had to face what was happening and deal with it. A last glance at the glorious sunrise and I headed back inside to start the process of cleaning this mess up. When I got downstairs, I noticed a pillow and blanket laying rumpled on the couch as if somebody had been sleeping there.

"Flora!" I called out, wondering where my aunt could be.

It wasn't like this was the kind of house you could lose somebody in. I heard a noise in the basement and frowned. What on Earth could she be doing?

I made my way carefully down the stairs to the basement. I'd only been down there once before and I'd learned pretty quickly that this area was in the same condition as the rest of the house. When I got to the bottom, I was shocked to find Conall in my basement standing in an awkward position as if he couldn't move.

"What's going on?" I asked.

"Somethings holding me here," Conall said through gritted teeth. "I don't know why I can't move."

I stepped forward and took a closer look, only to find black tendrils wrapped around Conall's leg.

"Do not move," I warned.

"What the hell is going on?"

I could tell whatever reason the sheriff came down here, he'd run into something there was no way he was expecting. "This house is cursed, and I think you just uncovered it."

Conall looked at me with an incredulous expression on his face. "Your aunt has you living in a cursed building?"

I shrugged as I knelt down by his side. "Who else could she have living here?"

Despite my earlier musings, I was shocked that the curse had been found. The last time I'd come down to the basement there had been no sign of it. Now there were literally hundreds of tendrils writhing around the floor and crawling up Conall's legs.

"What were you doing?" I had to still be sleeping because this situation was too weird not to be a dream.

"I came over last night because I needed to make sure you were okay. I thought I'd just sleep on the couch and we could talk this morning." He grimaced as he nodded towards a tool belt that seemed to have fallen to the floor. "I had trouble sleeping so I thought I'd do some work on the house."

"And you thought you'd start on my basement?"

I started wiping the tendrils off Conall's legs, but as quickly as I destroyed them, more came up from the floor to replace the ones that were gone.

"Flora suggested that getting a dedicated area set up might help your magic, and I figured I wouldn't disturb your sleep while I worked if I was in the basement." His voice trailed off. "It seemed like a good idea at the time."

I frowned. "Where's Flora gone? She was here when I went to sleep."

Conall inclined his head. "She left after I told her I was staying the night."

I wasn't sure how happy I was with that. I looked up at Conall and found a subdued expression on his face.

"Did you want to explain to me why the paramedics found you standing over the body of our football coach in the middle of the night with your ex-boyfriend?"

At this time of the morning I had to say that I really didn't.

"It wasn't a body. Coach Weber was going to be fine when he left here. I'm not sure what happened after that."

"And the ex-boyfriend part?"

"Julian has moved in next door. Flora and I needed help and we didn't trust that Hanlon would do anything about what's been happening in town lately, so we went to the magisters. Julian would only help if I agreed to work on the case with him. After the day we had, he wanted to keep an eye on me, so he was watching my property. When he heard the commotion, he came to see what was going on."

"Why didn't you call me?"

I could tell how annoyed he was by the vein that was ticking in his jaw.

"I did call you," I said quietly. "I left a message the day after you left, and you never called me back."

Conall stilled as my words got through to him. My relationship with Julian had ended when I opened my heart to him, and he'd left and broken off all contact. Before Conall left I had told him I was all in with our relationship. He had departed the next day to report to the Conclave and the Assembly, and I hadn't heard another word from him. I'd called him once, but when he didn't return that call I had felt like history was repeating itself. From Conall's expression I could see that he was getting it. Relationships were complicated and everybody brought their own set of baggage and trigger points. Mine was being abandoned, and he'd walked right into it. As a result, I had spent the last two weeks rebuilding the walls I had allowed him to breach.

I scrubbed my hands over my face. "Look, I don't have the time or energy to deal with this. I will get you out of this mess, and then I need you to be the sheriff and take control of this investigation. We've been working with the magisters in a vain attempt to get around the werewolves, but the process has been problematic. Now that Doug Weber is dead, we seem to have lost our best lead."

I went silent as I picked away at the tendrils and watched them disintegrate as I touched them. I thought my curse breaking ability had been getting stronger, but Coach Weber dying had knocked that belief. Uncertainty gripped me.

According to Flora, the curse on this place was strong. It had been dormant for decades, and now it decided to come alive. Maybe it could sense that I was not strong enough to fight it. I swallowed at the fear that Conall would be trapped and there was nothing that I could do.

"I'm sorry."

"What?" Caught up in my own self-destructive spiral, I'd almost missed the quiet apology.

"I should have returned your call. I made the wrong decision. I kept thinking that I should call you, but everything got away from me and I didn't."

I processed that for a moment. During the last two weeks I had entertained the thought that he might have got hurt or been unable to call me because he was on assignment or literally any scenario that was better than he just couldn't be bothered. I know that wasn't what he said, but that was what I heard. I couldn't even come up with a reply to that.

I glanced around the floor again and noticed that I had been having an effect and the number of tendrils was thinning. I also noticed that there was a writhing knot that had gathered around one particular floorboard. Abandoning my attempts at removing the tendrils from Conall, I started working on the pile. Underneath I found a short floorboard that didn't seem to quite fit with the others. Looking around I found a crowbar and I used it to try to lever the floorboard up.

"What are you doing?" Conall asked as he tried to pull his legs free.

"I think the tablet is under here. I just need to get this thing up.

I pushed again and the floorboard suddenly gave way. I dropped to my knees and used my weight to open more of the area up. I smiled when I found what I was looking for. In the cavity was a familiar stone tablet, wrapped in a piece of fabric which looked to be in the final stages of decay. I sat in the cross-legged position and got myself ready. I raised the tablet above my head.

"What are you doing?" Conall interrupted.

"I'm about to break this curse," I replied, feeling good for the first time in several days. Finally, I was about to accomplish something solid.

Conall frowned. "You need to get me out of here first. I can't help you if I'm trapped."

I looked towards Conall and whatever he saw in my face made the color drain out of his.

"I don't need your help. I've been dealing with this for the last few days without you. I'm sure I can continue."

I may have been a little harsh, but I was tired of people who didn't think I was worth the effort, and despite all of Conall's pretty words, that was what his actions told me. I lifted the tablet up and quickly threw it at the ground. Images slammed into me and I gripped my head. Despite the pain, I was relieved. Unlike what I'd been dealing with the last few days, this curse felt familiar. There was hate and rage surging through it. This was personal. I held on and coasted through the pain, only raising my head when I felt a hand on my cheek, and I looked up into pale blue eyes that were filled with remorse.

"Man, that woman was damaged."

"Who are you talking about?" Conall asked.

"The woman who put the curse on this house because of a will dispute. That was one messed up witch. I'm kind of concerned what else she did when she left here."

Conall stood up and I groaned as he pulled me up as well. In all the excitement I'd forgotten that I'd only recently been used as a punching bag.

"Sadie…"

I was saved from whatever he was about to say by a voice coming from the top of the stairs.

"Is anybody down there?"

I pulled away from Conall and headed in the direction of the voice. "We're here, Flora."

"What are you doing in the basement?"

I could hear the confusion in her voice and I had to smile because, despite all evidence to the contrary, today had started off as a good day.

I smiled when her face came into view. "I just earned the title deed for this house."

I had yet another shower, because there was no way I could face the world after what I had done this morning without cleaning myself up. I was pretty sure that I was developing some kind of psychological disorder around needing to clean myself after breaking these curses, but I was comfortable with that when the alternative was having the slimy remnants of evil attached to my skin.

I found Flora and Conall talking in low voices in my kitchen. I wasn't sure I liked the look on their faces.

"What's going on?"

Flora glanced at Conall and then looked back at me.

"I just received word from the doctor that Coach Weber did not die from the boils."

I frowned as I tried to remember if there was anything other than the boils on Weber's body. "What did he die of?"

Conall cleared his throat. "He was smothered at the clinic at about five in the morning."

I shook my head in confusion. That sounded too normal to occur in a town like Walker Bay. "Smothered? How did that happen?"

"We don't know, yet," Conall replied.

"Ambrose is furious," Flora added. "Nothing like this has ever happened in his clinic before."

I could imagine the doctor would be unhappy. "Are they suggesting I went down to the clinic and murdered him?"

That vein in Conall's jaw started ticking again. "According to Julian Bernauer he was watching you sleep through the glass doors of your bedroom at that precise time."

A smile crossed my face as I realized I had an alibi. It was a seriously creepy alibi, and Julian and I were going to have words over it, but if it meant I didn't have to go back in that jail cell, I was willing to overlook the disturbing aspect of it for now. That explained the unhappy look on Conall's face. I bet that wasn't a pleasant conversation for anybody to have.

"So, I'm free from suspicion?"

Flora inclined her head. "As free as you can be with Brigitte Hanlon in town."

That was a sobering thought. "So, what do we do next?"

Conall pulled out a chair and sat at the table. "Now I want a complete description of what has been going on in this town while I've been away, and nothing is to be left out."

Explaining what had been happening in Walker Bay took a lot longer than I expected, and by the time I'd finished, Conall looked as confused as we felt. He raked his hand through his hair. "So, let me get this straight. Lisa Atwill got lesions on her mouth from a curse on lip balm that she purchased three years ago. She had used that product previously with no problems. At the same time, Bryn Pritchard bought a cream that makes her nose look smaller and she's used it periodically over the last three years with no problems, but when you found it, there were those curse tendrils all over it, so if she had used it she would have got lesions on her nose."

"Probably," I commented. "Or it could have been something else equally unpleasant."

The sheriff grimaced and continued the summary. "Then the boys in the football team started being aggressive all of a sudden, and you say it was their championship rings, even though they've had those rings for several months with no hint of problems."

I was starting to see a pattern here.

"And finally, a bunch of people turned up at the clinic with those same lesions, and according to you they were affected because they touched some books in the library that were cursed."

I nodded.

"And finally, Doug Weber turns up on your doorstep affected by a curse that gave him boils. He starts to recover when you destroy the curse but is then smothered in his hospital bed."

I nodded. "He also admitted he had been doping the boys on the football team with a potion without their knowledge and that was why they won last season."

Conall frowned at that revelation. "I wish I could say I was shocked." He tapped a finger on the table. "Is that everything?"

I thought carefully. "Oh, and the assistant coach has disappeared. And Julian and I confirmed that Weber was having an affair with a witch out at the Albatross Inn."

Conall narrowed his eyes. "How exactly did you confirm that?"

I was no longer playing the game of trying to appease anyone. "We found a room which has an external door so he could hide his meetings with her. Julian then used his power which allows him to bring forth images of what has happened in the room. We watched Weber and the woman he was meeting, and the situation was just as disturbing as it sounds."

Conall leaned back in his chair and watched me. "I don't understand how this could happen all at once. Has somebody been going through town and putting curses on random objects? If so, why? What do the teenagers in town have in common with some books in the library. Is there a way for somebody to go into the coven library without your knowledge?"

He looked at me expectantly, but I didn't answer.

"Sadie, are you listening?"

I looked up at the concerned expressions on Flora's and Conall's faces. "When I first came to Walker Bay and we were looking for answers to break the curse on Flora, I remember walking past a book in the library and seeing a dark aura around it. I got Tilda to check it and she said there was nothing harmful in the book, so I figured it was just my imagination or the fact I was recovering from getting hit on the head."

I could see from the looks I was getting that they weren't following me.

"That book was one of the grimoires that I had to destroy. What if the curse was laid on these items in a way that they needed something else to activate them at a later time?"

I could see that Flora was picking up on where I was going with this. "You think that these curses were planted around Walker Bay, kind of like landmines, waiting for some instruction or trigger to go off together?"

I shrugged. "It's a theory. It would explain how the girls were able to use those creams for three years without any ill-effects. The boys have had those rings for a few months but it's only in the last few days that the aggression started. Except for the one book that caused me concern a few months ago, I would be willing to swear that there weren't any curses in the library during the time I've been librarian. All of these things have only happened in the last few days, like somebody has flipped a switch."

"Then how do you explain Coach Weber?" Conall asked.

"The curse was on a chain this Fausta had given him. We don't know how long ago he got it. It may have been activated at the same time as the others, or maybe she was afraid he would talk and activated it to stop him from betraying her," I replied, warming up to my theory.

"There is another question," Conall remarked. "Why, out of everybody in this town, did Coach Weber come to you when the curse hit him?"

I paused as that hit me. I was the last person Weber would want to go to. If he was looking for a witch to help him, the far better choice was the magister who lived just next door.

I focused on Conall. "I have no idea why he'd come to me. After our interview I figured he'd never want to see me again."

Conall looked troubled. "Is there any way he could know you're a cursebreaker?"

I shook my head. "Definitely not. The people I'm most worried about working out what I am are Dr Collias and Tilda."

"And the magisters," murmured Flora. "Julian Bernauer is focusing on you too much for me to be comfortable. The fact he lives next door is concerning. It might be worth us looking for a new place for you to stay."

I shook my head. "That is not going to happen. I finally got rid of the curse. There is no way you are moving me away from here now. This is my home."

I could tell that Conall wanted to argue with that announcement. Unfortunately for him, he didn't get a vote.

We were interrupted by my phone ringing. I should have

been more surprised when I heard Dr Collias' voice on the other end.

"I think we have another one," he rumbled.

"I'll be right there." I paused as I asked the question. "Who is it?"

I closed my eyes when he answered.

I looked up at Flora. "We've just got another case to add to the list."

"Who?" she asked, her voice filled with dread.

"It's Cleo Moore."

26

*B*etween my arrest and subsequent dramas, I had completely forgotten that I wanted to speak to Cleo Moore. I swore quietly at myself as the sheriff drove me to the clinic.

"It's not your fault," Conall rumbled. "You've done everything you could to get ahead of this."

"Yet, it's obviously not enough," I replied harshly. "They're only sixteen. What kind of sick mind does this to kids?"

"The world is full of people willing to hurt others for their own needs. Look at Doug Weber. He was so determined to keep his job that he managed to convince himself that it was acceptable to drug his team with a potion provided by a Traveler witch, without their knowledge. I knew he was selfish, but I never expected him to do anything like that."

Silence descended in the car. I was glad that Flora had chosen to see if she could get some information about Weber's Traveler witch instead of coming with us. There was no way I wanted anybody to witness the tension between the two of us. I hated this. When I first found out about the Destined Beloved prophecy, I was told it was like finding your soul mate. I thought that would make life easier. It didn't.

"I screwed up, didn't I?" Conall said softly. "I knew about your history with Bernauer. I should never have gone that long without contacting you. I've just never had to think of anyone else before. I'm having trouble getting used to it. I just figured I'd do my job and then come back, and we would pick up where we left off. I didn't expect you to be mad at me."

No way was he putting this on me. Something Julian had said came back to me. "Are you feeling trapped by this prophecy? If you are, I need you to tell me now so we can both walk away with a bit of dignity."

"This is coming from Bernauer, isn't it?" Conall growled.

"No, this is coming from the fact that the man I thought cared about me thinks it's perfectly acceptable to just not bother contacting me while he's away. You might not think it's important, but to me it is."

I threw open the door as Conall pulled up in the parking area. "And yes, you did screw up."

I stalked towards the clinic. I hated fighting but I refused to be with someone who was being forced by some magical prophecy that I hadn't asked for. I found Dr Collias standing at the reception area. Fortunately, for a change, it appeared empty.

"You rang?" I said curtly.

Collias raised an eyebrow and then I saw him look past me. Obviously Conall had followed, and from the look that crossed the doctor's face he had pretty much guessed where my bad mood came from.

"She's in here," he said, and I followed him down the hallway.

When we went into Cleo's room, I couldn't help my reaction. The poor girl had horrendous burns that seemed to cover her entire body.

"What...?"

The doctor shook his head and motioned me to follow until we got to his office. Once inside I turned to him

"What happened to her? That's not lesions, that is something different."

Collias nodded. "What she has are third degree burns. Fifty percent of her body is affected, and nothing we would normally do for burns is making any difference. I've had to sedate her. She is in so much pain."

"Did she say how this happened?" I couldn't even imagine what that poor kid was going through.

Collias went to the side of the room and pulled an object out of a drawer.

"She put this on her legs, arms and chin. All the places where she now has burns." He tossed a jar of cream on a table. "At worst she should have a skin reaction. No cream I know would cause something like this."

This cream would. It was crawling with tendrils. I had to fight to keep myself from retching, the nausea was so bad.

"I'll take it to Flora, and we'll see what we can do," I said.

Collias looked at me keenly. "I didn't think a cursebreaker required help from a mere coven leader."

I was impressed that I managed to not react to his statement.

"I'm a null, remember. Flora sent me to Arthur McClune because even she couldn't teach me."

"I believe that," Collias replied. "I also believe you're a cursebreaker.

Conall stepped forward as if to protect me. "Baseless accusations like that are very dangerous, especially with magisters around town."

Collias looked keenly at the two of us. "I'm not trying to hurt you and I would never betray your secret to anyone, but I am being inundated with curse victims and I can't fight that unless I know what weapons are available to me."

"Does it matter?" I asked.

"Of course, it matters," Collias said, his frustration obvious.

I shook my head. "No, it doesn't. You know that all you need to do is call us, and we are here immediately, willing to help. If we start putting labels on it, I may have to leave." I peered up at the man who three months ago I would have sworn could not possibly exist, pleading with him to understand. "I don't want to leave town. Please don't force that choice on me."

I waited with bated breath for the doctor's next words. I kept feeling like the veil between what people believed and what was the truth about me was becoming more and more flimsy.

"Very well," Dr Collias said clearly. "You're right, I shouldn't allow my curiosity to put anybody in danger. I'm sorry."

I gave him a small smile, relieved he wasn't going to push the issue and reached for the cream. "I'll see what we can do."

"How would we go about tracking down this Traveler witch?" I asked while I plucked stubborn tendrils from the jar.

After some consideration I had decided that I wanted to destroy this thing someplace where I felt a little less exposed. Cleo's reaction to the curse seemed more extreme than the others, and I had a bad feeling there was going to be a sting in the tail for this one.

Conall looked sideways at me, the only thing betraying the tension in the car were his white knuckles as he gripped the steering wheel. "Traveler witches generally live off the grid, and if they're using glamor it's impossible to keep track of them."

"How can that happen?" I asked. "I didn't think it was possible for anyone to really live off the grid these days."

"There's always a way," Conall replied. "You just need to be motivated and, considering the level of destruction this person is leaving behind, I'm guessing they're really motivated."

"It just all seems so random. I mean, think about it. What could possibly link the football team and people who use the grimoires in the coven library?"

Conall shrugged. "Maybe that's the point. A targeted curse only affects those who are hit by it. A curse that could hit anybody without warning for no discernible reason. That strikes fear into the heart of people."

I thought about that for a while. He was right. Maybe by looking for a link between the victims we weren't looking at the bigger picture. As we pulled up to the front of my house, I opened the car door. I turned when I heard Conall do the same.

"I've got this," I said. "You should go to the sheriff's office and try to get information from there. The assistant coach is still missing. We need to find him."

I could hear the growl in Conall's throat. "I know I screwed up, but you need somebody with you now."

I studied the car that was parked at the front of my house, looking anywhere but at him. "No, I don't. Flora's still here. If I need anything, she'll be the one to help me."

I closed the door and stepped away. I could see him struggling with his innate need to protect me, but that wasn't what I needed from him. I was beginning to fear that what I needed was something he was simply incapable of providing. Something in my face must have convinced him that I was serious because, with a final glance, he backed out of my drive and headed back to his office.

27

"*T*rouble in paradise?"

I swung around and took a wild swing, barely missing Julian's head as he jerked back. I pressed my hand to my heart, willing it to stop racing. "You are never to sneak up on me like that again," I hissed. "You scared the life out of me."

I surreptitiously slid the jar into the pocket of my jacket. The last thing I needed was for him to question what it was.

Julian held his hands up. "You seem a little on edge."

I pointed to my face which still showed evidence of my day as a guest of local law enforcement. "Is it any wonder?"

Julian's face darkened. "I can't believe that happened. I thought this was supposed to be a nice town."

"It is." I pushed my hands into my pockets. "What are you doing here?"

Julian reached out a hand as if to stroke my injured cheek. I lurched back and raised my hands. "Just don't. This is the last thing I need today." I stepped around him and headed towards my house.

"I thought you'd want to know that your grandmother

contacted me. She heard about yesterday and she's concerned about the environment you're living in."

I was wrong. This was the last thing I needed today. I stopped and turned around. "Next time you make one of your reports to Collette, you can tell her that her concern is noted but her opinion means nothing."

With that final word I stalked into my house and slammed the door shut.

"Do I even want to know?" Flora asked without looking up from her phone.

"No," I replied shortly. I pulled the jar of cream out of my pocket. And showed it to her. "Hair removal cream that managed to char the skin on a werewolf."

Flora winced. "I'm assuming it needs to be dealt with like the others."

Without answering I sat on the floor and crossed my legs. Taking a quick look around I spotted the fireplace. Considering how many cursed books I'd burned in there I figured that one more evil object wouldn't make any difference.

"This place is protected, isn't it? Nobody can tell what's going on in here, right?"

With Julian hanging around outside, the last thing I wanted was for him to be able to overhear what I was doing.

Flora nodded. "I have strengthened the wards on this place, although there seems to be an unusual aura to the house now. It feels like the house has a potency of its own that it didn't have before and that's fortifying the protective wards at a rate that I've never seen anywhere."

I knew it was ridiculous, but I felt a sense of pride at her words. Most people when they looked at this house only saw the decrepit structure, worn down by time, and what I now knew to be the toxicity of the curse that had been left to fester in its foundations. Now free of the evil, I knew she would flourish and protect me. I couldn't explain it, but I could feel it.

I looked over at Flora. "Just be aware, this might not be a pleasant one."

Flora grimaced. "When are they ever pleasant?"

She had a point.

"There seem to be degrees. Based on what I saw at the clinic, I've got a feeling this one has a bit more oomph to it."

I hurled the jar into the fireplace and watched as it disintegrated into dust. I wasn't prepared for what happened next.

A searing pain went through my whole body and for a moment I thought I was on fire. What was worse though was the emotion behind it, a repressed anger that terrified me. Before I blacked out a thought went through my head. Whoever was behind this was far stronger than I was, and sooner or later I might come up against a curse of theirs that I could not break.

I came to with my head in Flora's lap. "Told you it was going to be unpleasant," I mumbled.

"What the hell was that?" It was safe to say that Flora's normally calm demeanor was a little rattled. From the way her papers and phone were scattered around the room, my guess was that she'd moved fast when I hit the deck.

"That was what happens when prejudice and hate hide behind a wall of righteousness."

I pulled myself up and winced as every part of my body screamed in protest.

"I thought it would be like all the others that you destroyed this week. Why was this different to curses cast on Lisa and Bryn?"

I put my hand to my head. "Whoever did this has a problem with werewolves. They hide it behind wanting a return to the freedom of the past, but what they really want is to return to the times when witches held dominion over other paranormals."

"Great," bit out Flora. "Just what we need to add to this mess. Did you see anything else?"

"I saw another face but I'm pretty sure it was a glamor again. I'm beginning to doubt what I'm looking at. Is everybody able to do this changing their face thing? Because if so, I have some requests."

Flora shook her head. "Glamor is a very old and rare power. Very few witches have the ability to do it, and sustaining it is exhausting. Only the most powerful would be capable of even trying."

I guess that was something.

"What did you see, exactly?"

I pulled my scattered thoughts together and tried to focus. "I saw Cleo using the cream." I swallowed to get rid of the lump that had formed in my throat. "I saw her burn."

"Is there anything you can tell me about the Traveler witch?" Flora asked urgently.

I shook my head. "A description is useless seeing as she isn't showing her real face. All I can tell you is what I'm feeling from her. She really does not like this town, or the people in it." I was reminded of something a rogue witch told me about Walker Bay once. "She wants to see the town burn."

I dropped my head as my phone started ringing. Both Flora and I looked at it without moving. After being exposed to so much hate, I really didn't feel like talking to anybody. What I wanted to do was have a shower and scrub myself clean, and then crawl into my bed for the next few days. Unfortunately, that did not look like it was in my future. When the phone stopped ringing, I breathed out a sigh of relief, only to use some choice words when Flora's phone started. Being the coven leader, she couldn't be quite as selfish as me.

I only barely registered her low voice as she talked, my mind racing. The worst part of breaking curses was the incomplete images that raced through my mind. Sometimes they were horrific and at other times they were mundane. Rarely were they clear.

"Cleo's going to be okay. The burns have started healing."

I looked up at Flora, my mind barely registering what she had just said.

"That's good. Nothing else has come in?"

Flora shook her head, her expression worried. "Are you okay?"

I nodded and then shook my head. "I need to take a break. That one hit me hard."

I felt disjointed and confused, as if I was here with Flora, but also somewhere else.

"I just need a break."

I know I told Flora that I needed to rest, and in my defense I really tried, but after an hour of not being able to quiet my mind, I figured I'd give up and get something to eat. That was how I found myself in the diner, ordering a burger and wondering who in this town was going to get hit by the next curse. The sheriff was right. The very randomness of these curses was an effective means of causing terror. Most of the town weren't aware of what was going on. It was only a few of us who knew. That had to mean something. I tilted my head as I contemplated the problem.

"What are you doing?"

I grinned at Tilda as she watched me warily.

"I'm following a thought that isn't making sense," I replied.

"It looks painful," she said as she sat down. "Anything I can help you with?"

I really wish she could. "No, not today."

She put her hand gently on my arm. "Are you okay?"

I started at the question. What did she know?

"Everyone's talking about what happened to you while you were in jail. I tried calling but Flora said you needed time to rest and heal."

I could see her distress at the thought that I might think she was neglecting me, but to be perfectly honest, I was so focused on the curses that were happening around town that I'd managed to push it to the back of my mind. Compartmentalization was an amazing thing.

I gave her a comforting smile. "Flora was right. I just needed some time to deal with everything." I could tell I was a bit subdued for Tilda's liking, but I was feeling really strange.

"Word is the sheriff turned into a berserker and rescued you." Tilda couldn't help her excitement and I understood. I just couldn't deal with it right now.

"Can we talk about something else? Anything else? How's Lisa doing?"

Taking the hint, Tilda rolled her eyes. "Grandma's gone into over-protective mode and any moment Lisa's going to lose her mind. I'm just waiting with the popcorn for the fireworks to start."

You're not sounding very sympathetic," I remarked.

"At least it's not me."

I was about to make a comment when my attention was taken by who was coming through the diner door. Tilda twisted around and swore as she saw what had caught my attention.

"You have got to be kidding me."

I was just as shocked as she was. I figured Detective Hanlon would have quite a lot on her plate at the moment, what with a murder and the abuse of a prisoner in her custody. It seemed I was wrong. I could not believe it when she stepped up to our table.

"Despite the protection you seem to have, you are still a

suspect in the Coach Weber murder case," she hissed, her face twisted with anger.

"Really?" I replied a lot more calmly than I felt. "I was pretty sure I had a cast-iron alibi."

"You do," rumbled Julian.

My attention had been so focused on Hanlon that I hadn't noticed the three magisters walking up behind her, but I shouldn't have been surprised. I didn't seem to be able to turn around these days without a magister being right there.

"You've got guts, if nothing else," drawled Julian, his eyes focused on the detective. "My understanding is that you've been ordered to stay at least a hundred feet away from Sadie. I don't think the coven advocate will react well to you talking to his client. I believe he's relishing the opportunity to pin your hide to the wall, and he's got your boss at the State Police on speed dial at the moment."

I could see Hanlon wanted to react, but she knew she couldn't. She'd overreached in arresting me, and the attack by Rogers pretty much sealed her fate. It would take a miracle to save her career now, and she knew it. Julian thought that threat would make her back off. I knew it just made her dangerous.

Without a word, she turned on her heel and walked away. Julian looked at me expectantly. If he thought I was going to invite him to join us, he was sadly mistaken. Out of the three magisters, Liam was the only one who stood a chance, and despite how fond I was of Tilda, I really didn't feel like his company today.

With no invitation forthcoming, Julian nodded and headed for a table at the back of the diner. Before she followed the others, Magister Hartford lowered her head next to me. "You got what you deserved," she whispered before walking off.

I wish I'd been more surprised at the venom in her voice.

"She's a piece of work, isn't she?" Tilda remarked.

That was the polite way of putting it.

"Have you and Flora gotten any closer to finding out what happened with Lisa?" Tilda surprised me with her change of subject.

I leaned back in my seat. "We're working on it. I just don't understand why anybody would do that."

Tilda watched me keenly. "I heard Cleo got affected by the same kind of thing."

There was no way they were close. Horrible as Lisa's curse had been, Cleo's had been next level torture.

"Cleo seems to be doing better now." I dodged the question I could see in her eyes. "Dr Collias is keeping a close eye on her."

I could see my answer wasn't what Tilda was looking for in the way she screwed up her nose.

"What did you and Flora…?"

Her voice dropped as a figure stepped up to our table and grabbed my arm. My first instinct was to pull away, but when I looked down, I saw a hand covered in boils and my heart sank.

"Help me," the voice moaned, and I looked up into the ravaged face of the assistant coach, Peter Martel.

As I stood up, he fell to the floor and the hoodie that had been covering his face slid down, exposing a sight that wouldn't look out of place in a zombie movie. I dropped to the floor beside him and Tilda followed me. The noise around us rose as people started noticing that something was seriously wrong.

"What's going on?" The fear in Tilda's voice was palpable. I couldn't blame her.

"I don't know," I lied. I knew exactly what was happening. The tendrils crawling up Peter Martel's arm were a fair indication that we had yet another curse on our hands.

"Somebody call an ambulance," I yelled out, hoping somebody actually would call an ambulance and not expect one of the other bystanders to do it.

This was my worst nightmare come to life. If I didn't break this curse now, Peter Martel was going to die. It didn't take a genius to see that. But we were sitting in the middle of the busiest place in Walker Bay with everybody watching. I felt exposed, but I had to make a choice. Was my secret worth his life? As the assistant coach moaned in agony, I knew the decision had been made for me. I started wiping down his arm, dislodging as many tendrils as I could until I found the source of the curse. A leather cuff on his wrist proved to be the culprit. I looked around quickly as I tried to work out what my options were. The magisters had taken on the role of crowd control and Julian squatted down beside me.

"What's he doing here?"

I loved the way he thought that I would have an answer to that question. "I don't know. How far away are the paramedics?" Maybe if I could get a ride in the back of the ambulance with Martel, I could deal with the curse there, when I didn't have dozens of eyes watching me.

"It's coming but it's going to take some time. It was on another call."

I closed my eyes. That was not good.

"Can you get a first aid kit?" I asked hoarsely. In truth, a first aid kit wasn't going to help one little bit, but if I was going to do this in front of everybody, I did not want Magister Julian Bernauer right behind me.

When he left to find the kit, I took in a deep breath and made my move. I really did try to be discreet, but sleight of hand was simply not one of my gifts, and with Martel having a death grip on me, I fumbled as I pulled the leather cuff off his wrist. I knew Tilda saw what I was doing and there was no way I could account for all the eyes watching the scene in front of them. The best I could hope for was that the situation was so chaotic that nobody was watching me closely enough to understand what was going on.

I gripped the leather cuff in my hand and hoped this was not one of the curses that sent me unconscious, because I was never going to be able to explain that away. With my head bent so nobody could see my expression, I curled my hand over and crushed the cuff. Of course, I couldn't be lucky. Pain streaked through me, and it took every ounce of willpower to stop me from screaming out. I couldn't get a grip on the images I was seeing but I could tell this curse was connected to all the others. As the pain died down, I was left with a clear impression of triumph. Despite my breaking it, this curse had accomplished its purpose. I just wish I knew what that purpose was.

I breathed through the lingering pain and was surprised when I felt a hand rubbing my lower back.

"It's okay. I've got you."

Despite my anger with him, I had to admit that knowing that Conall was with me gave me a sense of relief. I looked over my shoulder into his pale eyes that were filled with concern. "We need to get him out of here."

Conall nodded and stood up. "I need everybody to get out!" he bellowed.

In no time the diner was cleared. Tilda gave me a regretful look as she obeyed Conall's direction, and I could see Julian resented the order but knew he had to go. Conall went to pick Martel up, but the pain-ridden man refused to let go of my hand. Deciding that carrying him with me attached was going to be too difficult, he pulled the man to his feet. Fortunately, Martel's strength seemed to be returning and he was able to move slowly to the front of the diner. Conall pushed Martel into the back seat of his truck with me being dragged along behind.

"What happened?" Conall asked harshly as he navigated the streets of Walker Bay.

"I don't know. He just walked up to us while we were eating."

"You, specifically?"

"Yes."

"That's not good," he said quietly.

Tell me something I didn't know.

By the time we reached the clinic, Peter Martel was beginning to show signs of recovery. His breathing became more regular, the boils were looking less angry and he showed signs of alertness. When Conall came around to help him out of the truck, the death grip on my hand loosened.

"Thank you," he whispered.

29

*T*hanks to the fact that I had already done the heavy lifting in this case before we turned up at the clinic, it wasn't long before Dr Collias had declared the assistant coach was no longer in danger and we were able to talk to him. I stood at the side of the room, trying to be as unobtrusive as possible. I don't know why I bothered. Peter Martel did not take his eyes off me the entire time he spoke to the sheriff.

"Do you know who did this to you?"

"Fausta," Martel replied quietly.

"You've been involved with the same woman that Coach Weber was having an affair with?"

Martel nodded slowly.

I couldn't help the irritation that I was feeling. Did nobody in the werewolf clan take their vows seriously? If they wanted to play the field, they should never have got married in the first place.

"Do you know why she did this?"

Martel shook his head and I could see the beginnings of

tears in his eyes. "I loved her. I would have done anything to protect her. Why would she do this to me?"

Conall glanced over at me and I nodded in response. I didn't know whether these two men would have been predisposed to having an affair, but I was willing to bet that they had been dosed with a powerful love potion. Nothing else could explain this level of devotion to a woman willing to kill them.

"Were you aware of the doping of the kids on the football team?"

Martel hesitated for a split second. "Of course not. How could you think I would do something like that?"

Even I could tell he was lying.

Conall raised an eyebrow. "Because I've known you my entire life. Winning is all important and nothing else matters." He leaned forward and I could see the fear in Martel's face. "Now, somebody just tried to kill you, and unless your wife found out what you've been doing behind her back, I am quite confident that it is because of what you did to those kids. I would suggest that unless you want to suffer the same fate as Weber, you come clean."

I started when I saw real fear in the assistant coach's eyes. "Nobody was supposed to get hurt. It was just supposed to improve their strength and speed. It wasn't even doping. It was more a supplements program."

I felt sick at the way he tried to justify what he and the coach had been doing.

"Who instigated it?" Conall's voice was calm, but I could tell from the tight way he held himself that he was furious at what the two men had done.

Martel looked up and I could see the shame in his eyes. At least that was something.

"Weber suggested it to me early in the season when we were losing all our games. We decided to test it first and see if it worked." He paused as if trying to work out how to present the facts in the least incriminating way possible. "Once we determined it didn't harm the kids, we continued to administer it to them in a careful manner."

Translated that meant once they started winning games they just kept going, regardless of the effect on the kids.

Conall leaned back slightly as if giving him room to speak. "What exactly did you do?"

Martel swallowed and looked away. I figure it was easier to confess when you didn't see the growing censure in other people's eyes.

"Fausta had a potion that she said would help the kids be better versions of themselves. It was clear and most importantly it didn't taste like anything. We put it into the team water bottles for training and games." His eyes swung between the two of us as if begging us to understand. "We were really careful with the dosage. The kids were never in any danger."

I could see the disgust Conall couldn't hide, and I was pretty sure I had the same expression on my face.

"Where can we find this Fausta?" Conall asked.

Martel shrugged helplessly. "I don't know. She would call me when she was in the area and I never knew when that would be." He swallowed. "That was the exciting part. The anticipation. I've never known a woman like her."

If he was lucky, he'd never meet another. He gave Conall a description of Fausta, but I knew it didn't mean anything. The fact her glamor was that of an intoxicating beauty meant nothing. Her actions told us what she was really like.

"Where did the championship rings come from?" I asked.

Martel shrugged. "The boys were presented with them when we won."

"So Fausta didn't give them to you to pass along to the boys?"

Martel shook his head.

"Was there any point where she could have got hold of them before they were presented to the team?" I persisted.

Martel frowned as if he was trying to think hard. "The ceremony to present the rings was held at the school a week after the game. There was some delay. I don't know what it was. I figured the supplier was just running late."

It was more likely that Fausta needed time to get hold of the rings and curse them.

"Where have you been the last couple of days?" Conall asked. "We've been looking for you."

"I was waiting for Fausta. She told me that she wanted me to meet her at an old fishing cabin we would…" His voice trailed off as if he knew we would be able to fill in the blanks. "She never turned up."

"When was the last time you saw this Fausta?"

Martel frowned. "Not since before the championship game."

Conall started. "You mean, she hasn't been anywhere around Walker Bay for months?"

"No. Weber and I had been trying to contact her, but we couldn't find her anywhere."

"Why did you go to the diner when the boils started?"

Martel looked at me. "I was told the coven leader's niece was the only one who could help me.

My breath caught in my throat. There was no way anybody could know that, unless they also knew my secret.

"Who?" Conall asked, fear lending an urgency to his voice.

Martel shrugged. "I don't know. I was heading back to town when I fell, and someone came up to me. I couldn't see them properly. It looked like a ghost, but they told me where she was and that she was my only chance to live." He looked over at me. "I wasn't going to hurt you. I just needed help."

I nodded at him, unwilling to trust my voice. Somebody else knew what I was. I felt like I couldn't breathe. Without a word I slipped out of the room and headed towards Collias' office. The doctor was standing behind his desk and looked up in surprise at the way I burst in.

"Did you tell anyone?"

"What…?"

"Did you tell anyone about your suspicions about me?"

Different expressions crossed the centaur's face. Annoyance at the interruption, anger that I would question his integrity, and finally compassion for the fear that had obviously gripped me. He walked around the desk and grasped my shoulders.

"I have not betrayed you, not in thought or deed. I value what you have done. The last few months would have been carnage without your assistance, and I will be forever grateful that you found your way to us."

Those gentle eyes were my undoing and I started crying. I felt him enfolding me in his arms and I just let it all go. I wasn't strong enough to handle all this and I could feel myself falling apart. I seemed to have this permanent disjointed feeling, like I was existing in a separate realm to the people around me. I didn't know if it had something to do with the curses I'd been breaking or the stress of the situation.

I felt myself being turned around, and I knew that Conall had walked in and I'd been passed along. I felt his lips on my hair and heard him saying a lot of nonsensical things. He was swearing that nobody would be able to hurt me, but I knew differently.

*a*fter my breakdown at the clinic, Conall had taken me home and organized for Flora to take care of me while he hunted down the reason for my fear. I'd never seen so much rage coursing through him, and I'd been there the day he'd almost killed his brother to protect me. I was too worn out to argue. All these curses coming at me at once was doing something, and I was very afraid that it was damaging me in ways I couldn't comprehend. When Flora had walked into my house, I could see she had the same fears. She gave me a potion that she swore would help me sleep and I crawled into bed, my one thought being that I really wished my mother was still here. I desperately needed to talk to her.

Yet again I woke up to sound of pounding. I threw off my quilt and headed downstairs. I didn't care if I was being arrested again. I was sick of people banging on my door as if they were trying to knock it down. I yanked open the door, ready to yell at...nobody. That couldn't be right. I looked around my porch, and I was right the first time. There was nobody knocking on my front door. That noise had to come from somewhere. I shut the door and jumped when the pounding started up again, but this time I could tell it wasn't coming from my front door. I sighed as I realized it was coming from my basement.

"What are you doing?"

Conall straightened. "I'm repairing the floor in here. You did a bit of damage when you were looking for that tablet."

"I meant why are you doing construction work on my house at this time of the morning," I grated out, determined to get my aunt to remove that exemption that she'd put in the wards around this house for my Destined Beloved.

"You love this house," Conall said.

I nodded sharply. I had no idea where he was going with this, but everybody close to me knew how I felt about this house. It was the first place I had ever lived in that I had started thinking of as a home.

"You're about to run. I can see the signs. If I can turn this place into a home for you, then you might decide to stay."

Okay, now I was getting confused. I sat down on the bottom step, hoping it was stable enough to take my weight.

"I don't understand what you're talking about."

Conall sighed and ran his hand through his hair. He dropped down on the floor next to me and took my hands in his.

"I can see the signs of somebody about to run, because that's where I was a couple of weeks ago. I didn't realize it at the time, and I was fortunate in that I could hide it as a job I had to do."

He was right. My last thoughts before going to sleep had included a long road trip out of town.

"I'm really bad at this relationship stuff," he said, and I could tell from the look on his face that he was finding every moment of this conversation to be absolutely excruciating.

"You scare me."

I frowned at that statement. "How could I possibly scare

you? You are literally the most frightening person in this town, and that includes the trolls."

Conall looked down at me. "You don't realize how necessary you have become to me in a short space of time. When I think of you not being in my life, I can't breathe. I'm trying so hard to do this right, but I just know I'm going to screw it up. I already did." He ran his hand through his hair. "I've never needed anyone like I need you. That thought terrifies me. I haven't dealt with it well. When I went to make my report, I figured it was a good time for me to ensure that the Destined Beloved prophecy was real and not some weird magical addiction."

"So, you went cold turkey," I murmured. "That was stupid."

Conall nodded, a wry smile on his face. "I don't like not having control of my emotions. I wanted to have that control back."

"How'd that work out for you?"

Conall tipped up my chin so he could look me in the eye. "I was miserable, every moment away from you. I saw your face everywhere and I wanted so much to hear your voice, but my need for control got in the way. I will never let that happen again."

"How can you be sure?" I asked.

"Because while I was away I realized that I love you," Conall replied.

My mouth dropped open. To say that I was stunned was an understatement, but then reality reared its ugly head.

"It's the prophecy messing with you. At some point you'll realize that this whole thing is magic and you're trapped." I hated the fact I was echoing Julian's words.

Conall shook his head. "Before I left, I knew you were necessary to me. Having the time apart made me realize I was in love with you, not because you're my Destined

182

Beloved, but because you are brave and caring and loyal, and you inspire loyalty from others." He waved a hand in the air. "Pike even likes you, and believe me, he doesn't like anybody."

He held my hands and looked deeply in my eyes. "I don't think the prophecy is making us feel this way about each other. I think it was just letting us know what was inevitable so we'd find each other sooner. I truly believe that even without the prophecy we would have got here anyway."

I closed my eyes and swallowed. "Those are pretty words, but you've said pretty words before. You still walked away from me."

Conall nodded. "I did and I am so sorry for causing you pain. I didn't intend to. I can now say with certainty that I will never do anything that stupid again."

"The problem is I don't know if I can trust that. You've done it once. What stops you from doing it again?" And I really couldn't deal with it if he left me again.

"You're right." Conall looked around as if searching for an answer to my question. "Then marry me. That way you know I won't leave."

I snatched back my hands. "Are you insane? There is no way I'm going to marry somebody just to ensure he stays with me."

Despite my extreme reaction to what should have been a romantic moment, Conall smiled. "I'm not suggesting we do it to force me to stay. I want you confident in me and my commitment to you. My actions have shaken that confidence. Getting married is the only way I can see that changing."

"No," I said, shaking my head. "I won't marry a man until I trust him completely." I looked at him sadly. "I don't trust you."

I hated that I hurt him, but it was the truth. He had his

reasons for doing what he did, but I was struggling emotion-
ally at the moment. Until I was in a better place, I wasn't
making a commitment to anyone.

Conall drew in a breath. "I understand."

"That's good." I stood up and wondered how you were
supposed to act after a rejected marriage proposal. I was
pretty sure retreating to our respective corners was the best
thing to do, so I gave him a quick nod and abruptly headed
up the stairs. I should have known Conall wouldn't leave it at
that. When I reached the kitchen, I heard him follow me.

"So, I have to win back your trust."

I spun around. "What?"

"I love you. We are literally destined to be together. I
broke through that wall you've got built up around your
heart once. I can do it again."

I was not sure I liked the look in his eyes. He looked like a
man with a mission, and based on what I knew of the sheriff,
he did not accept failure.

Fortunately, my phone chose that moment to ring, and I
blindly grabbed it off the counter.

I frowned when I didn't recognize the number, but I
needed something to break the tension in this room, so I was
willing to risk answering the phone to a telemarketer.

"Hello?"

"Sadie, is Tilda with you?"

I stiffened at the tearful voice. "Lisa, what's wrong?"

"Grandma got hurt. I need Tilda and I can't find her."

"She's not with me. What happened to Maude?" I couldn't
help the urgency in my voice.

"I don't know," sobbed Lisa. "I heard her scream and I
came downstairs and she had burns all over her arms. I
called the ambulance and they've taken us to the clinic." She
paused and I heard muffled voices in the background.

"Sadie?"

I closed my eyes when I heard Dr Collias' voice.

"Is it another one?" I whispered urgently. I could see the worried look in Conall's eyes.

"She has burns similar to Cleo."

"Is it a cream or is she wearing some kind of jewelry."

I could hear the doctor questioning Lisa.

"No," he said when he came back on the line. "No cream, no jewelry. According to Lisa, she was about to make breakfast when she started screaming."

That didn't help at all. "You know the drill," I said, weariness swamping me yet again. "I'll see whether I can find what's causing this."

I put my phone down and turned to Conall. "I need to go to Maude's house. Looks like another one."

He swore loudly and creatively. I had to admit that I wholeheartedly agreed with the sentiment.

*G*etting into Maude's house was a lot easier than I expected. Most witches had wards on their house which either prevented intruders from getting in, or did something particularly nasty to them when they breached the perimeter. The wards Flora had put on my house instantly encased the intruder in crystal. Fortunately, most law-abiding witches had an exemption that allowed first responders to enter in an emergency situation. Having Conall with me saved me from a potentially unpleasant situation.

"Where should we start?" Conall asked as he opened the door.

"Lisa said she was making breakfast when she started screaming. I guess the kitchen is the best place to start," I said as I headed in that direction.

I stopped suddenly at the doorway.

"You see it?" Conall asked.

You'd better believe I could see it. I stepped closer to the kitchen counter and started wiping away at the pile of tendrils that gathered there. At the touch of my hand they started to disintegrate. As I wiped them away the medium for the curse came into view and Conall stepped forward to get a better look.

"Somebody cursed a cookbook?"

I could understand the incredulity in Conall's voice. Considering the effect casting a curse had on a witch's soul, it seemed to be overkill to do it on a cookbook. Once I'd cleared all the tendrils, I studied the book I'd found. Just like all the other objects it was normal. Completely and utterly normal. I shook my head. Spending time contemplating the futility of cursing a cookbook was a waste of time when Maude needed the pain to stop now.

Before I'd left home, I had put together what I was going to call my rudimentary curse breaking kit. I put the small bag on the table and pulled out some lighter fluid.

"Do I want to know?" asked Conall.

"Probably not," I replied, before tossing the cookbook into a small fireplace that I'd spotted in the kitchen and liberally coating it with the lighter fluid.

"You're going to set the house on fire," the sheriff commented, his tone showing an understandable concern at my actions.

"I hope not," I said fervently.

I lit a match and flicked it into the fireplace, taking the time between flicking and ignition to step backward and sit on the floor before I fell. Behind me, I felt Conall take position as if ready to catch me. For some reason everything seemed to happen in slow motion. The cookbook seemed to be fighting the fire, unwilling to succumb. I watched as the flame struggled and I willed it to catch. With a sudden whoosh the flames caught and the screaming in my head started. This time it wasn't just Maude's scream I heard. There were screams coming from the curse of hostility and rage. Whoever had cast this curse had hated Maude with an intensity that was breathtaking. I held it together, breathing through the pain as the flames consumed the cursed cookbook. As the ashes settled, I felt something I had not expected to feel. I felt triumph, and it wasn't coming from me.

"You okay?" Conall had moved closer to me and his body heat warmed me against the cold feeling going through my soul.

"Something's wrong," I replied. "That one was different."

I leaned back against him, hoping to draw in some of his strength, and he wrapped his arms around me.

"I'm sorry," he whispered. "I can never explain how sorry I am for leaving you like that. All I can say is I swear it will never happen again."

I could hear the sincerity in his voice and I let go of some of my anger. It wasn't doing me any good, and I was afraid that it was combining with the effects of the curses and messing with me. I gave myself a moment to enjoy the feel of him with his arms around me, but I knew that it couldn't last.

I slowly pushed myself up. "We need to contact Dr Collias."

Conall pulled out his phone and passed it to me. In moments I had the doctor reassuring me that there was some improvement in Maude's condition. From our experience with Cleo we knew that it would take a little time for the burns to fully heal.

"I need you to ask Maude about a cookbook she was using this morning. I need to know whether she bought it from a Traveler witch and when she bought it."

I waited patiently while the doctor asked Maude the question.

"Sadie?" I could hear the concern in Dr Collias' voice and I was instantly put on edge. "Maude was given that book by her mother when she got married."

I frowned. That couldn't be right. "Are you sure? It was the one with the old building on the front and some pretty purple flowers."

"She's sure."

"Has it ever been out of her house? Has she ever let anybody borrow it?" I knew I was sounding desperate, but this wasn't making sense.

"She has lived in that house since she got married at eighteen years old and that cookbook has not moved from her kitchen."

I closed my eyes. That was not good. "I'm coming to the clinic." We needed to talk this through, because if that book had been in this house for up to fifty years, then how did it get a curse on it?

I turned back to Conall, knowing that I didn't have to tell him what was going on thanks to his werewolf hearing. "We need to go, now."

I stopped as a small movement caught my eye. I stepped over to the sideboard and found one tendril wrapped around a small jewelry gift box.

"What is it?" Conall asked.

I picked up the box and watched as the tendril disintegrated. Opening it I found the box was empty. My stomach plummeted as a really bad feeling went through me. "We need to get to the clinic, now." I snapped the box shut and hoped with everything I had that the panic racing through me was misplaced.

As we pulled up to the clinic, I was surprised to see Eamon. "What are you doing here?" I asked as I got out of the sheriff's truck.

"Checking up on Martel," he replied. "We've had a guard

on him to make sure the same thing that happened to Weber doesn't happen to him."

That made sense. A quick glance over at Conall told me that he was fully aware of the werewolf clan taking care of their own. I wondered how long that protection was going to last once the clan found out he'd been doping their children with a witch's potion. I had a feeling the sheriff was going to need to step in at that point.

"What are you doing here?" Eamon asked as he fell into step beside me, his tone conversational but I could see his eyes were sharply evaluating.

I didn't have the werewolf sense of smell, but I was pretty sure that Eamon was going to be able to catch the scent of lighter fluid and fire around me. No wonder he was curious.

"Checking on Maude," I said. "She got burnt in the kitchen today."

I could see that didn't make sense to Eamon, but I didn't have the ability to make up a plausible explanation. Especially when I saw Lisa in the hallway outside her grandmother's room.

"What is this?"

Lisa looked shocked at the abruptness of my tone, as I shoved the jewelry box in front of her, but that bad feeling in my gut was increasing exponentially.

"It's Tilda's."

My heart sank. "When did she get it?"

"Liam gave her a pendant last night. She wanted to show it to us, so she brought it over before they went out."

"Did she put it on?"

Lisa frowned at what she obviously thought was a stupid question. "Of course, she put it on. It was beautiful and Liam's been so good to her. He said last night was going to be special and he wanted to mark it with a memorable gift."

I felt the tension in Eamon as he stiffened beside me.

"Were you able to get in touch with Tilda?"

Lisa shook her head. "I figured she spent the night with Liam."

I didn't have time to worry about the way Eamon winced at that statement. I pulled out my phone and tried ringing her. It rang out. I was about to try again when a video call from Tilda's phone came through.

"Thank goodness, Tilda. I need you to come to…" I stopped talking when I saw Liam's face. "Hi Liam, where's Tilda?" I asked, not liking the look on his face

"Hi, Sadie. I was wondering when you'd start looking for your friend. You've seemed so occupied lately. I know Tilda's been feeling a little neglected."

I forced myself to breathe normally as the sound of his voice grated on me. "I was just going to see if Tilda wanted to join me for breakfast. I'd love you to come as well. It would give us a better chance to get to know each other."

"That would be great," said Liam, "but I'm afraid Tilda's not really up for breakfast, at the moment."

My breath caught as the video was turned around. Tilda was lying on the ground, tears streaming down her face, black tendrils wrapped around her neck. They seemed to be squeezing and letting go, allowing her to get a breath before just as quickly taking it away. It was as if the curse was torturing her by keeping her on the edge of death.

I used a few choice words to describe Liam's parentage.

"Now, now," said Liam, mildly. "That's not the sort of language I would expect from a Harstone."

Then it was a good thing I was a Goodwin, because according to the upbringing I'd had, that was an entirely appropriate response to this situation.

"You are going to tell me where she is," I threatened.

"Of course, I'm going to tell you where she is." Liam sounded surprised that I believed he wouldn't. "She's in the clearing near the river that passes by the coven library." He lowered his voice. "I'm not going to insult anybody's intelligence by insisting you come alone, because I am aware that the berserker would never allow that to happen, but you need to know that if you are not the first person to step into this clearing, she will die and it will not be a good death."

With that chilling warning ringing in our ears, he cut the connection.

The second the video call ended, Conall and I were heading for his truck. The sheriff was on his phone, organizing deputies to meet us at the clearing, and I was focusing on all the parts of Liam Rigby's body I intended to dismantle the first chance I got. I wasn't surprised when Eamon got in the truck with us.

Conall jerked his head at Eamon who looked like he was going to lose that famous Tolan control. "What's wrong with him?"

I shook my head. If he hadn't worked it out by now, I wasn't going to fill him in.

Despite the impatience I was feeling, it didn't take long for us to reach the coven library where Karl and Pike were waiting. While the sheriff filled them in, I pulled Eamon to one side.

"I need you to hold it together," I said quietly. "We need answers, not a dead magister."

"And if killing him is the only way to save Tilda?" Eamon snarled.

"It isn't," I said, confidently. "I have a feeling I'm going to be distracted so I need you to focus on her. Make sure she's safe. Don't risk her by going after him." I could see Eamon struggling with my request. "Please."

That was all it took. "Okay. Just, take care of yourself too. Tilda's the bait. He wants you."

I swallowed. I was all too aware of that.

"You ready?" Conall looked at me strangely as I'd activated my troll doll to protect Eamon's privacy.

I nodded. "Remember, I have to be the one to step in that clearing first." I put up my hand as I saw Conall about to argue. "That's non-negotiable. I won't lose Tilda because of your overprotectiveness."

Conall hesitated and then reached for me and pulled me to him. "Please, don't get yourself killed."

I gave him a tiny smile and kissed him quickly. "Same goes for you."

I pulled out of his arms and started heading for the clearing. It didn't take long for us to reach it. The ease with which this place could be found told me more than anything that Liam had a plan.

As I stepped into the clearing with two werewolves, an ogre and a dwarf close behind me, I noted two things. Tilda was on one side of the clearing, gasping for breath. Eamon made a beeline for the young woman, his features tortured as he pulled at the necklace which was slowly strangling the life out of her.

On the other side of the clearing was Liam. Normally, you would think he was slightly insane to still be here considering the firepower I'd brought with me, but I could see a shimmer in front of him. I picked up a rock and to the shock of my friends, I threw it straight at him. A foot away from his body it bounced off what seemed to be a transparent shield that completely surrounded him.

"That wasn't very nice," he said, his handsome face now twisted into something I barely recognized.

"Neither is using your girlfriend as bait. I'm here now, just like you wanted. Stop hurting her."

Liam paused as if thinking. "No. If you want to save her, you need to do it."

And there it was. I had no choice. I strode over to Tilda and knelt down next to her, pushing her hair back.

"You're going to be fine. Trust me."

I started pulling at the tendrils. I didn't think about the fact that my secret was being exposed. All I thought about was the friend who had always treated me with kindness from the day I met her. As I destroyed the tendrils, those that remained kept squeezing harder. They were no longer giving her any chance to breathe. I doubled my efforts and cleared the last of the tendrils away, ignoring the frantic whispering that Eamon was doing, desperately trying to keep Tilda from slipping away from us. I grasped hold of the pendant hanging at Tilda's throat and crushed it. As the images hit me, I was surprised how clear they were. They showed how Liam had inserted himself in Walker Bay by seducing one of its most popular members. I couldn't believe the cynicism and ruthlessness he'd shown in his pursuit of Tilda. All so we could get to this point. I could also see that Tilda now knew how he'd used her. That was going to hurt her for a long time. The worst part was feeling the emotion behind the curse. It wasn't rage and it wasn't hate. It was pure naked ambition. I opened my eyes to find Eamon consoling Tilda who was now breathing and sobbing as if her heart was breaking.

I grasped her hand and put my other on her cheek. "You're safe now. He is never going to hurt you again."

"Well done, Harstone. You truly are not what we were expecting. Who would have thought that the null could be a cursebreaker?"

I turned to face the mocking voice behind me. I could see the sheriff and two deputies taking up positions around the clearing.

"Why are you doing this?" I cried.

Liam smiled. "It was a test, and you passed, or failed. It depends on your point of view."

My heart seized. "What do you mean, a test?"

"We knew somebody in Walker Bay was interfering with our plans, and it could only be a cursebreaker. I've been setting off these curses, hoping to narrow down who it could be. This was my final proof."

He pointed behind me and my mouth dried when I saw a camera positioned high in a tree, pointed straight at the clearing.

"Don't bother trying to destroy it. The camera is streaming the video to a server very far from here." He gave me another of his smiles. "I'm not the only one with access to that server."

"Why? Why all these curses attacking Walker Bay? They didn't accomplish anything."

"They helped us discover you, didn't they?"

I glanced over and saw the panic in Conall's eyes at that statement.

"You did all this just to find me?" I couldn't believe the crushing guilt I felt as I thought of the pain inflicted over the last week. Then a thought struck me. "Most of the curses were on objects that came into the victim's possession before I even came to town. There is no way you could have known about me back then."

Liam tilted his head. "You're right. We didn't know about you, but Walker Bay has always been a center of power. It was inevitable that a cursebreaker would find their way here. Curses have been seeded around this town for years, just waiting for the day that they could be activated. Think of it as a minefield. Using just a few of the more benign ones to flush out a cursebreaker seemed to be a fair trade. They were already here. They just needed to be triggered. That was my job." He grinned. "Of course, we were lucky in some cases. Did you enjoy the resurgence of the curse in your house? I wish I'd been able to see it. It would have been satisfying."

That explained some of the curses, just not all of them. "Who created the curse for Tilda?"

Liam turned his glittering eyes to me. "It was my privilege to create that curse."

I heard Eamon growling and had a feeling Liam had just signed his own death warrant.

"Who is Fausta?" I asked desperately.

"Fausta is the leader we've been waiting for."

"You don't know who she is, do you?" I guessed. "Despite all you've done for her. You've sold your soul for her, and she still doesn't trust you enough to know who she is."

I could see Liam's anger growing as I taunted him. I could also feel Conall's tension as I made the murderous psychopath angry.

Tilda screamed as the four men were suddenly picked up and flung to the ground. I could see them trying to get up, but it was like they had boulders on top of them, pressing them down.

"Stop!" I screamed.

"Did you really think I was staying here to be caught," Liam sneered. "You have the information you wanted. Now you have to make a choice. We know you haven't been able to access any powers. You will never be able to find what you're looking for in this town. Come with me and I will take you to people who can hone your abilities. You will become the strongest cursebreaker to ever live."

I croaked as I laughed at him. "You are joking, aren't you?" I shook my head. "You have caused pain to the people I care about. Do you honestly think that I would ever align myself with people who are willing to do that?"

I heard a groan from behind me and dropped to my knees beside Conall as he struggled valiantly against an unseen force. "Let them go."

"No."

I looked over at the man who thought that threatening the people I cared about was the way to win my loyalty.

"Agree to come with me and they will live."

I knew that wasn't the truth. No matter what I decided, everybody in this clearing was going to die. Liam and the people behind him had worked for too long on this plan of theirs to relinquish the secrecy now.

I stood up and faced Liam, anger surging through me. I could tell from the arrogant look on his face that he didn't think there was anything I could do to him, but there was something he didn't know. Every curse I had broken had left something with me. I had dealt with this by compartmentalizing the hatred and the rage, keeping it away from the core of my soul. Now I was facing a situation where I needed to be more than a cursebreaker. I couldn't be the passive shield anymore. That wasn't going to protect those I loved. I needed to use this power of mine in another way.

Without giving any thought to the consequences of my actions, I started breaking open every compartment in my brain that I had used to deal with what had happened over the last couple of months. I tapped into Isobel's ambition to lead the coven, no matter what it cost her. I felt Jeanette's naive arrogance as she used a curse she couldn't control to try to enslave two of the strongest werewolves in town, and I felt Ilsa's rage as she took revenge on Walker Bay for the death of her daughter. Mostly, I felt the indescribable hate and anger of the witch who had decided to destroy Walker Bay by manipulating it from afar. All of this power and rage stirred inside me and I felt something push out and head for Liam.

The horror on Liam's face when that power punched through his shield like it was nothing was something that I would never forget. Up until that moment I could tell he thought that nobody could touch him. He was wrong.

As I heard Liam's agonized screams, a moment of clarity hit me. This wasn't me. I looked down at my hands and in my mind I could see the tendrils that I feared so much attaching themselves to me. That was why so many cursebreakers ended up turning to dark magic. You spend so much time dealing with evil and you start losing an important part of your soul. That's what had been happening to me these last few days. It's why I had been feeling so strange. My soul had become tainted with every curse I broke, and the darker my soul got, the more powerful I became. Powerful enough to be useful to somebody determined to bring about an apocalypse.

I looked into the faces of Karl and Pike as they pulled themselves to their feet now that Liam's hold on them was gone. These were men who had become my friends and who I could see even now refused to condemn me for what I was doing.

I glanced over at Tilda who looked like her world was coming to an end. She didn't even notice that Eamon was holding her up, determined to support her as her heart splintered. From the expression on his face, I had a feeling he was planning on staying there.

I swung my head towards Conall. Regardless of our recent difficulties, I could still state with absolute confidence that he was the best and strongest man I knew. A man who had every reason to give up, stood beside me, prepared to lay his life on the line for me if that was what I needed. He wanted to marry me, and even though I wasn't there yet, I could see the possibility of that future. A future I may be destroying this very second. I took in a shaky breath. That was the life I wanted, and if I was going to get it, I had to start today and resist the temptation to blast Liam Rigby into oblivion.

I took a deep breath and remembered something my mother had told me when she was teaching me how to drive. She told me that when I went into a skid, don't look to where the car is going, look to where you want to end up and your hands would guide the steering wheel in that direction. I pulled my eyes away from a writhing Liam and pushed it towards a group of trees, only to watch them disintegrate to dust. I fell to my knees and saw Liam do the same. Conall rushed to me and clasped me in his arms.

Karl ran to the magister and, before he could recover, rolled him over and put cuffs on him as if afraid the magister would regain his bearings and release an unimaginable power on us. He needn't have worried. After what I had just unleashed on Liam, he was going to need a long recovery time.

"Are you okay?"

I looked up into Conall's caring eyes. "No, I don't think I am."

was surprised to see Tilda making her way across my deck. After we'd left the clearing, we'd dropped Eamon and Tilda off at the clinic and Conall had brought me home. The decision had been made that after the revelation of my true nature, it was only fair to give Tilda a chance to be in a stronger place before dealing with me. Seemed Eamon was just as overprotective as Conall.

I winced at the angry red marks that streaked her neck. "I am so sorry that happened to you."

Tilda put a hand to her throat. "I sure know how to pick them, don't I?" She sat down next to me and looked out over the sunset. "This is a beautiful spot. Pity the house is such a disaster."

"It won't be for long." I took in a deep breath and activated the troll doll, knowing that my future in this town hinged on the next few minutes. "Flora let me stay here because it had a curse. She said if I got rid of the curse, I got to keep the house."

"You broke the curse," Tilda said carefully.

I nodded but was careful not to look at her. "It looks like

it was one of the curses triggered by Liam. It trapped Conall in the basement, so I had to get rid of it."

"The plague was a curse, wasn't it?"

"Yep."

"And the curse on Flora?"

"Breaking that one was an accident," I pointed out. "When I came here, I had no idea that I could do something like that."

"And that's why Flora has been teaching you." She frowned as a thought came to her. "Did you trap Isobel?"

I had to choose my words carefully. "After I broke the curse on Flora, Isobel found us. She was about to cast a stronger curse on the both of us. I stepped in front of Flora and it's like I was a shield. It bounced back on her."

"Could you break it?"

There was a question that had been torturing me for weeks. "I don't know. I'm guessing the answer to that question is yes."

Tilda fell silent and I waited patiently.

"When we approached that cottage on Henrietta's property, you saw something."

I nodded. "There was a curse surrounding the building. Anyone who crossed it would have started hallucinating before finally going insane."

"You stopped me from crossing it but couldn't tell me what was going on." She sighed. "Sorry I got so angry with you."

"Perfectly understandable." I lowered my voice. "I'm sorry I didn't tell you the truth."

Tilda gave a sad smile. "Not exactly something you'd be able to share easily."

We lapsed into silence as we both gazed out over the bay.

"Eamon said he loves me."

I blinked in surprise. That was quick, and probably the

worst thing he could have done. Aidan must have seriously damaged his sons when they were growing up. They did not seem to have a clue when it came to navigating relationships.

"How do you feel about that?"

Tilda snorted as if trying to suppress an inappropriate giggle, and surprised me by laying her head in my lap as she stretched out on the deck. "Well, Dr Goodwin, I'm feeling confused. The man in question has never been on my radar and I just got my heart ripped apart by a magister." She frowned. "You warned me about that."

My warning about magisters hadn't even come close to covering what Liam had done.

"Maybe you should just be friends to begin with," I suggested.

"Yeah," she drawled. "He seemed a little intense today. I'm not sure he'll cope with being friend zoned as well."

I hated to agree with her, but I could see her point. "Just do what's right for you."

Tilda got a faraway look in her eyes and I could see fear clouding them.

"Are you going to be okay?"

She shook her head as if trying to dislodge some bad thoughts. "I'll be fine," she whispered. "I don't want to go home. All I see is him and the way he looked as I was slowly being strangled to death."

"Would you like to stay here?"

I saw a flash of amusement in Tilda's eyes. "In this death trap? No offense, but I'm going to stay with Grandma and Lisa." She pulled herself back up to a sitting position. "I just wanted to make sure you and I were okay before I went to their place for the night."

I nodded and got swamped with a hug. Tears started welling in my eyes. I hadn't been able to admit to myself how terrified I had been that I would lose her friendship now that she knew my secret.

I heard a throat being cleared. "Is everything okay?"

I looked up to find the sheriff watching us, concern etched into his features.

Tilda sniffed. "We're good, Sheriff."

Conall watched warily as Tilda hugged me again and made her way across the deck. She patted his chest. "Don't worry, I'd never betray her."

Relief spread across his face and he dropped down next to me as we watched Tilda leave.

"I didn't expect you here so soon," I remarked.

"Conall shrugged. "What Liam did went beyond a local matter. He's already been snatched up by the Assembly before the Conclave has time to act.

"Where did he end up?"

"The Assembly has him stashed away at a black site. He's being interrogated to find out who is behind this. Once they've got all the information he can give, he'll go to trial for the murder of Doug Weber and for the assaults on various people using curses. He'll never see the light of day again."

"So, he did kill Coach Weber?"

"Yep, that was the one thing he did admit to before we transferred him. When the curse didn't kill Weber, Rigby sneaked into the hospital and smothered him. He seemed to relish boasting about such a hands-on killing. I'm guessing there's a screw loose in that man's mind. It's a pretty good bet that if he'd been born in the normal world, he would have still been a murderer."

"Did he say why Weber came to my house or who Fausta really is?"

"He refused to give us any other information, but I'm pretty sure that it was all part of this test of his." Conall looked down at me, his concern obvious. "Somebody else knows your secret, and they're going to come after you. We need to come up with a plan."

"Tomorrow." I just wanted one more night where I could pretend to be normal. "What about the Conclave? Won't they object to the way this has been handled?"

"Whoever is behind this has to be involved with the Conclave somehow. They're not going to tip their hand by protecting him now, and those that aren't involved won't want to be seen to be supporting someone who deals in curses."

I didn't know much about the Conclave, but I had a feeling their willingness to stay on the sidelines was not going to continue.

"I need to tell you something."

I stiffened at the tone in this voice.

"The last two weeks I've been doing work for the Assembly. There are rumors that there is dissent in the Conclave. A faction is building and it is gaining power. Talk is of a leader who will usher in a golden age of witchcraft."

"I'm guessing that doesn't bode well for the rest of the world."

Conall shook his head. "Throughout history, it is very rare for a group to achieve eminence without stepping all over everybody else."

I leaned my head against his shoulder and Conall tucked a stray piece of hair behind my ear. I just wanted to sit here and let my cares flow away. Unfortunately, my brain wasn't willing to stick with the program.

"I can hear those wheels turning. What are you thinking?"

I sighed as I tried to make sense of what was going through my head. "If we hadn't been able to break these curses, what would that have done to Flora's standing in the community?"

Conall frowned. "She would be seen as ineffective. In a

disaster, the leaders are always the first to be blamed. Sometimes it is deserved. Sometimes it isn't."

By the widening of Conall's eyes I could see he was following my train of thought.

"And when leaders become ineffective, communities start looking at replacing them, either through democratic means or through a coup." I really didn't like where I was going with this.

"Coven leaders don't get voted in," Conall murmured, his hand stroking my arm.

"So, we could be looking at a coup?"

Conall sighed heavily. "I think that's the least of what we're facing."

I looked out across the bay. I had a bad feeling he was right.

ABOUT THE AUTHOR

Leonie Gant started her writing career at the age of ten when she stuffed notes in her pencil case full of ideas for mysteries that Nancy Drew and the Hardy Boys should really have been solving. After years of watching mysteries play out in her head she decided that writing them down was the best way to deal with them.

In her life away from writing, she is a voracious reader with not nearly enough time to make her way through all the books she wants to read. She also enjoys bushwalking, sewing and chocolate, possibly not in that order.

To find out more about Leonie Gant and her books

www.leoniegant.com

DISCOVER OTHER TITLES BY
LEONIE GANT

The Harstone Legacy

Curse the Dark

Curse the Soul

Curse the Heart

Curse the Past

Not in Hollywood

Not Famous in Hollywood

Not Happily Married in Hollywood

Not Talented in Hollywood

Not Wanted in Hollywood

Not Suspicious in Hollywood

Not Forgotten in Hollywood